The Attunist

Gary B. Haley

Other Titles in the Attune Trilogy

The Attunement

The Attuned

The Attunist

Gary B. Haley

No A.I. Certified:
The Attunist is an original work of intellectual property, and has been certified by NoAICertified.org to be free of input from any kind of artificial intelligence.
Certificate # 20221215GBH

ISBN:
9781957218014

Publisher:
Have Coffee Will Publish
(www.HaveCoffeeWillPublish.com)

Editors:
Ines Kirkpatrick
English professor, library director and world class editor.

Rhonda Lee Carver
Editor extraordinaire and award-winning author.

Contributing Editor:
Have Coffee Will Edit
(www.HaveCoffeeWillEdit.com)

Pre-Release Proofreaders:
T.K. Lukas
Best-selling author.

Jane Whitmeyer, Megan McCauley and Natalie Soine
Accomplished proofreaders for multiple (grateful) authors.

Printed in the USA
Second Paperback Edition

Table of Contents

Foreword...ix

Weeks Later 1

Three Campfires, Three Layers 5

Coasting..9

It Never Ends 11

Chip's Down 19

Back in the Game 21

Better Bitter than Broke.....................................27

Sweet Ride 29

A Campfire in the Sand 35

To the Cenotes 41

Come UP with a Plan?...47

Ds and Fs 51

Ants and Undies 57

Come Up with a Plan 63

On the Trail Again 65

Chaos..69

Wait, What? 71

For-E-ver...73

Moving On..75

Brothels and Borders 79

From Chris-Craft to Chris Cross..........................83

Coincidence or Catastrophe?.............................87

Surf's Up...89

Miami Bound..97

Snooty Does Not Mean Refined.........................99

Pointing North...101

Kids Are Expensive 103

Inside Information...105

Rocky Mount..107

Froggy...109

SO Close! 113

Atlantic City 115

Dunking the Scone 117

And the Kitchen Table...119

Diamonds Are an Outlaw's Best Friend 121

Gratuitous Yelling C.O. 125
Tourist Traps and Diamonds 127
Focused on Revenge 133
Bright and Surly...135
Legal Now...137
Philly Stakeout 139
Still Catching Up 141
Streetlamp Shadows 143
Another Interrupted Lunch 147
Locked Eyes 149
Bricks and Sugar 151
Playing Spoons 155
Just Handle It...157
Bottom Rung 161
Next Rungs 165
Yes, Ma'am! 173
Three! Two?! 177
A Chip Off the Old Anonymity..183
Who *Are* You? 191
Patience of an Ambush Predator 195
Take Him Out or In? 197
Carla's Folder, Ken's Task..203
Egos and Solutions 207
The American Dream 213
Well, Okay Then 215
Roger That..219
I'm Taking This Laptop 223
Old School DOS Prompt 229
(°°°) 233
The More You Have..237
No Questions Asked 239
Quite the Agenda 247
Into the Sunset..251
Afterword...259
As the Credits Roll 261

Foreword

The Attunist is the last book of my Attune Trilogy, which is based on the adventures of an IT Geek who became an effective vigilante, and the FBI agent who helped him. Over the years, they would occasionally call or meet me in and around Denver to catch me up on their latest endeavors. Sometimes their stories involved taking out entire terrorist networks. Other times they had focused on disrupting the flow of illegal drugs into the United States. I never knew what to expect.

In the first two novels, I did my best to disguise places and events to help keep the two of them anonymous and safe. Those stories are *similar* to what actually happened. This novel is a little different because of its nature. Many of the places, events, and people are described with more accuracy.

I'd like to include a personal note here to explain why we need the next section of this Foreword, which is a recap of the first two novels. I've never done this before, preferring to make each novel in a series a standalone experience, and they are according to most readers. However, the most common criticism people make when reviewing books in a series is, "I'm not sure I know everything I'm supposed to know."

On behalf of authors everywhere, I'd like to make a friendly suggestion. If you are kind enough to take the time to leave a highly-coveted review of a book, please understand that if authors included full character development in every book in a series, there would be far more unfavorable comments than the few we get from people reading sequels before prequels. So, rather than making uncomplimentary remarks about a lack of redundant character development, may I suggest reading the prequels before posting a review?

Independent authors do not make a lot of money on book sales, even when we sell thousands of copies. Most authors barely make a profit at all when you consider all the time and resources we put into writing a book. The cost of editors and traveling to the locations we write about is substantial, but we want to get details correct. Also, with each novel, I spend hundreds of hours on research, hoping to provide an authentic experience for readers.

Converted to a common standard, indie authors probably average about fifty cents per hour. We're not in it to get rich. Most of us write to simply share our stories and thoughts.

When authors ask people to consider reading prequels or sequels, it is less about making another sale and more about encouraging readers to enjoy the complete story.

So! Below is the recap, which is the last section of this Foreword. If you don't want to know, or already know, skip this and dive right into the first chapter, "Weeks Later."

Recap: Spoiler alert! This section contains spoilers for both The Attunement and The Attuned.

The Attunist refers to someone who became attuned to the fact that we humans can control a specific wavelength of energy that is produced by our brains. When birds and mammals are exposed to this particular wavelength, their nervous systems become temporarily disrupted and cease to function. When their brain is exposed to high concentrations of that wavelength, the usual outcome is instant death. Lights out. However, when arachnids and possibly insects are exposed to the same wavelength, it only agitates them.

The Attunist uses his ability to control this energy to take out criminals and terrorists. Some people choose to call this capability a "superpower," which might be interpreted as not being based on reality. But if you look at any common electroencephalogram (EEG) you'll see evidence that the wavelengths exist.

And *yes*, all you DoD and Pentagon lawyers. I removed references to the wavelength and frequency from this manuscript, even though what I had included were *not* the actual values. (FYI: While writing this short paragraph, I mumbled "jerks" too many times not to mention it.)

Sorry, had to vent. Back to the recap.

To clear up any confusion about The Attunist's name, and why it is not in the first two novels, he and Carla simply chose not to share that with me. That is fine, of course, given the nature of their situation and what writers typically do with the information they have.

Special Agent Carla Bright is an FBI agent who felt morally compelled to help The Attunist stop some exceptionally dreadful criminals from hurting and killing innocent people, including children. While working together, Carla and The Attunist learned to truly respect each other and eventually fell madly in love. They happen to be a good match.

Chip Granberry also has special abilities that some people insist on describing as a superpower but is simply an exquisitely fine-tuned sense of intuition. Pretty much *every*one has a sense of intuition, he just learned to use his better than anyone else. He crossed paths with The Attunist and they became friends, but immediately after Chip introduced him to his girlfriend, Shannon, she disappeared.

Shannon Williams (an alias she had created) is a mystery, too. Growing up, her father was a con man. The last time she had heard from him was several years prior to meeting Chip. Shannon had long since distanced herself from her father because he was still running cons. It was his way of life. He had included her and her brother in his scams as soon as they were old enough to memorize their parts. They often had to flee in the middle of the night and move to a town in a different state. He would reinvent himself there, and create new identities for his family. The man is currently incarcerated, after being arrested for stealing from the elderly.

Eventually, Shannon landed in the tiny mountain town of Bristlecone Springs and met Chip. When he introduced her to The Attunist at a poker tournament, he asked her if he knew her from somewhere. This spooked her into hiding and the calamity crushed Chip into depression.

Detective Alparslan "Al" Kemal was an enigmatic conundrum in the first two novels. Bad guy? Good guy? Indifferent? Turns out, he was a good guy, although a little rough around the edges at times. Most people like the guy, despite his lack of higher interpersonal skills. He works for INTERPOL in Turkey and has one of those angry bosses who yells *every*thing.

Qian is a young terrorist from China who managed to survive when The Attunist killed Qian's fellow "professors." Qian's colleagues had called The Attunist "Sciens" which added to his intense hatred and blinding lust for revenge. Despite being the youngest faculty member, and because of his privileged upbringing, Qian thought *he* should have had the title of Sciens, which was the highest tier at their "university." Also, Qian never even considered that The Attunist had acted in self-defense when he killed the terrorists and many of the students in the mob that had chased him.

Jeanna Doyen, a struggling single mother, met The Attunist when they were co-workers at a research company. When a terrorist attack caused that corporation to fold, he created a small business and hired Jeanna to run the operation. She excelled in her role and made the company so successful that he made her a co-owner, but then he mysteriously disappeared for months. In his absence, she reluctantly accepted a buy-out offer to prevent a hostile takeover of the business and put his share of the money, $3M, into a trust fund. Then she found out her business partner, and friend, was considered a serial killer. This left her confused and angry, often wondering if her life, or the life of her precious son, were ever in danger.

Nurmuhammet Mammetgeldiyev, better known to some by the nickname "Dunlap," befriended The Attunist in a time of dire need at a terrorist training campus in Turkmenistan. Dunlap only knew The Attunist by the title Sciens, which had been given to him by the leaders of the campus. These "professors" had lured him there to try to recruit him, but after an altercation, The Attunist killed the group of international terrorists and fled from angry students in an attempt to spare their lives.

Dunlap followed The Attunist, assisted in his escape, and then helped him out of a nest of scorpions early the next morning. He then hid his Sciens in his grandmother's hut near the middle of the village where he was born.

The people of Dunlap's village felt indebted to The Attunist for shutting down the terrorist training camp in the mountains above their village, so they helped him. Dunlap's grandmother nursed and fed Sciens until he recovered from his wounds and a nasty scorpion sting. When The Attunist recovered enough to walk, he began the long journey home but left a relatively large amount of money in their hut.

Weeks Later

Clean, secluded beaches like the one before me are rare. I could not see another person in either direction or a single ship on the hazy horizon. To my right, in the distant southeast, I could see the coastal town of Coatzacoalcos. I'd guess a mile and a half to two miles away. Rhythmic, Gulf of Mexico waves crashed onto the pristine sand in front of me, and behind me was a rocky waterfall cascading down the twelve-to-fifteen-foot cliff I had slid down to get to the beach.

Palm and cypress trees, myrtle, and a thick underbrush of ferns, holly, and ivy were perched atop the overhanging cliff. Seagulls swooped and mewed. Smaller birds ran up and down the surf, snatching tidbits from receding waves. Tiny crabs darted back and forth, competing with the smaller birds for nourishment while fleeing from the gulls.

A fine mist blowing off white-capping waves cooled my skin and carried with it the soothing scent of saltwater.

"This'll do."

Dropping my backpack, I sat in the sand. Tourist-shop quality seashells were everywhere. The Gulf breeze, the shade of a palm tree, and a bottled water finished cooling me down after a long hike. It was a huge relief to pull my shoes and socks off my aching feet.

I'd been walking all over Mexico for weeks and had lost track of the date, but figured it was late January. Thanksgiving, Christmas, and the New Year had come and gone, barely remembered. No family, no Carla, no turkey, no dressing, and no pumpkin or pecan pie.

Being a fugitive wanted by several law enforcement agencies is as solitary as it sounds.

The life I had created for myself was not the greatest, but I took comfort in knowing my efforts had made the world a slightly safer place for others, and for future generations.

A solar charger for my cheap, burner phone had been a good investment. I plugged it in and propped the photovoltaic pane in the sand. It didn't take long to have enough power to check my email, voicemail, and the news, but today was no different. No one had called and only spammers emailed. They don't care if you're a fugitive, as long as you buy something.

Thankfully, I found I was no longer in the news. Social media, THE media, and therefore the world, had become bored and moved on to other stories, as they do.

The calming sounds of the beach lured my thoughts away from my past and the circumstances that led me to this moment. What did it all matter, anyway?

I wish Carla was here. She would love this beach. I pulled a photo of her out of my backpack and took a long look. *Miss that girl.*

Rested and hydrated, I placed her photo into a pocket of my backpack, rolled my pants legs up to my knees, and walked the short distance to the waves. The hot sand massaged my feet and the soothing sound of curling waves partially drowned out the painfully constant ringing in my ears.

With the noticeable reduction in the ringing came the disturbing memory of the incident that had caused my hearing loss. A violent and prolonged gunfight in Iran. I was unarmed except for my special abilities, which were rendered useless by the solid rock banks of the ravine where we took cover. The terrorist cell that ambushed us had been armed with fully automatic weapons and hand grenades, so until Carla managed to grab one of their AK-47s, it had been her and her trusted GLOCK against an army.

I touched the scar on my right forearm where a searing hot bullet had ripped through my flesh and bone that day. I slid my finger back and forth through the length of the divot. When I pressed deeper, I could feel the depression where the piece of bone had been blasted away.

A wave rolled up the shore engulfing my ankles. The cool temperature of the water surprised me and began pulling my mind out of the past again. The vivid memory was hard to shake, but I cleared my thoughts and waded in. When I was in up to my knees, a synchronized school of small, gray fish swam around my legs. They parted into two sections to circumnavigate the two obstacles in their way, but then immediately reunited on the other side. I watched them continue on in unison through the clear water until they parted again around something else in the water.

What is that?

When the school of fish shimmered away, the reason for their behavior became obvious. A jellyfish! I scrambled out of the water, turned around, and looked out into the surf. There were several more out there, floating around with beguiling innocence. Beautiful and graceful, and deceivingly dangerous. Not far away, another was dead in the sand.

It's no wonder this beach is deserted.

Undeterred by the jellyfish, a sea turtle swam by. When it was gone, I turned and moved away from the crashing waves, disappointed about not being able to enjoy the cool water.

Piles of driftwood lined the shore near the cliff, clearly marking the limits of high tide. I gathered several stacks for firewood in a recessed part of the cliff, under some overhang. The recess in the cliff face was deep enough to hide my fires unless someone walked by on the beach. Soon, I had three campfires cracking and blazing. The smoke stung my nostrils a little, but the aroma of the burning driftwood allowed me to slip into a state of tranquility.

"Blissful" came to mind. Tranquility. These mindsets are difficult to achieve when you're wanted by the FBI and several terrorist organizations, but there I sat. Peacefully. Not worried in the least about being arrested or killed. Blissful.

Until sunset, when mosquitos and sand flies appeared and made life unbearable.

This won't do at all.

Three Campfires, Three Layers

I took all the clothes out of my backpack and put them on. Three layers, including some that needed laundering. This helped deter the insects, but having only short-sleeved T-shirts, I was still miserable. I moved over to sit with my face in the smoke of one of my campfires and placed my hands under my arms, which helped enough to prevent insanity. Over the past few weeks in Mexico, I had spent every night under the stars, but nothing came close to this agony.

Oh, for a nice hotel. Or a cheap motel.

Only the morning sunlight forced the insects to retreat. Exhausted from the long night, I stood, stretched, and removed my extra layers of clothing. I drank my last bottled water as I walked the beach into Coatzacoalcos. Near the hotels and resorts there were sunbathers, but few people were in the surf.

At a couple of different stores in the coastal town, I bought mosquito netting, bug spray, several citronella candles, some throw lines for fishing, a machete, a roll of duct tape, and two large rolls of twine. From a street vendor, I picked up several bottles of water and three tacos that may have been the best I had ever tasted.

The rest of the morning was spent several yards into the untamed forest atop the cliff that overlooked "my" beach. I found a section of a creek where the water was moving rapidly over cascading waterfalls. Two old cypress trees growing on opposite banks had thick branches that met over the creek, making a perfect place for the base of a treehouse.

Using my new machete, I cut down enough sapling trees to build a platform above the creek, lashing them together with the twine. It took most of the day to get the floor stabilized in a way that allowed the trees to move in the wind without ripping the structure apart. The base was too rough to sleep on, so I piled on enough coconut hair, ferns and elephant ears to make my new bed as comfortable as possible.

When the setting sun began summoning all kinds of vicious, bloodthirsty insects, I hung the mosquito netting over a forked branch and lit two of the citronella candles inside the mesh tent for a short while. After I blew out the candles, I fell asleep listening to waves playing on the beach while a cool ocean breeze flowed through the trees, but then something rare happened. I slept all night.

A croaking sound woke me, and I was pleased to find orange, eastern skies dimly illuminating the forest. Best alarm clock ever. As the croaking continued, I realized it was coming from the trees, not the ground. Tree frogs? Catching some movement in the shadows, I realized they were not frogs, but toucans. Toucans! I watched them bounce around in the branches while the sun crept up over the Gulf of Mexico.

Huh. I have an odd craving for Froot Loops.

Nothing but time.

I cut more saplings and elephant ears to use to build a rainproof, overhanging roof. When I saw a band of spider monkeys move through the area, I added sturdy walls and a door. A vine and twine ladder made it easier to get up and down, and some camouflaging made it impossible to see unless you were close.

Fresh coconut for breakfast. Crab for lunch. Fish for dinner, and coconut water straight out of the shell made for a refreshing treat any time. Dropping red hot rocks from the campfire into coconut shells full of water from the stream provided all the drinking water I needed.

My days were repetitive, but not boring. A stunning sunrise woke me every morning. Warm-to-hot days were spent exploring my beach and the surrounding area. Watching the sunset every evening soothed me and warm nights listening to the waves helped me sleep. Sometimes it rained, but I didn't mind. I added a solid roof over my treehouse so I could enjoy the storms, too.

Nothing but time.

My new home was nothing like my family's old cabin in the Rocky Mountains, but the results were the same. Peace and tranquility. Although sometimes I missed Carla so much I couldn't even stand myself. The last time I saw her, she had been trying to arrest me. I wasn't sure she had a choice in the matter, but someday I intended to contact her to find out. After things had some time to cool off, of course.

Arrest warrants had completely derailed my life.

Coasting

Carla paddled her way through the steady stream of cases that flowed across her desk. She paced herself according to the amount of work assigned to her. She didn't try to advance upstream, but neither did she allow herself to be carried away by the current. She simply performed her due diligence, even though her heart was no longer in it.

She had helped someone that her FBI colleagues considered a serial killer, yet somewhere along the way had fallen madly in love with him. She had joined the joint task force team that was on their way to arrest him to protect him. When they missed him by minutes, she felt sure he was watching them.

She hoped he didn't feel betrayed by her, but instead, recognized her true intentions. That might prove to be difficult for him though, knowing she had also helped the FBI confiscate his cabin in Colorado, which had been in his family for more than a hundred years.

With the help of a large team, she had learned that he had gone from squeaky clean, without so much as an unpaid parking ticket, to the man she knew who routinely killed drug dealers and wiped out entire terrorist organizations. Carla knew law enforcement *needed* someone like him, although she also realized there was no legal way to allow him to help.

During the long course of their investigation, someone on her team had finally discovered his real name, but she had not seen him or spoken to him in a long time. Not since she and Detective Kemal had unwittingly abandoned him in a hostile environment in Turkmenistan almost eighteen months ago.

Carla was having a hard time believing that.

Eighteen months? Has it really been a year and a half?

It Never Ends

Since I was old enough to venture outside by myself, I have loved exploring nature, so I often wandered through the thick forest northwest of Coatzacoalcos. Usually, I followed my creek upstream to see what I could find.

One warm day in February, I hiked up into some nearby hills and noticed a small valley between four rounded peaks. The valley was covered in knee-high grass but only sparsely dotted with trees and bushes. In the middle of the valley, under the shade of a single tree, I could see a semi-circle of dark gray stones protruding from the grass. I hadn't seen any other circular rock formations in the area, which made me wonder if fellow humans had carefully arranged the placement of the stones, or if it was the rim of an ancient volcano.

A closer inspection revealed frightful faces carved into the stones, arranged so they were facing the point that would have been the center of the circle. The rocks were weathered, but the faces were still clearly recognizable. I pulled grass away from the statues, discovering that each head had a body. Some were holding spears or knives, while others carried what could have been farming tools and plants or seeds.

This has to be Mayan. This entire valley, tiny as it is, should be an official archeological site.

I visited the site every day or two, cleaning the leaves and grass off the statues and away from the base of each, being careful not to disturb the stones or anything on the ground around the find. I also did my best to determine the exact coordinates of the valley. I wanted to inform someone of my find after I vacated the area. The statues had been there for centuries though, so it wouldn't matter if I took a few days to take photos, make some notes, and enjoy being an amateur archeologist wannabe.

Sometimes I sat where all the statues were staring to see if anything magical or out-of-the-ordinary would occur. It didn't, but I wasn't disappointed. I examined the ground under that same spot, but did not see anything. I didn't dig there, of course, because I had no idea what might be significant.

On another warm, windy morning, while exploring a new part of the forest, I crossed the dirt road leading to Tecuanapa, which was a mile or so away. Not far from the road, I happened across a small field of coca plant sprouts. They were planted in a meadow that was, roughly, about a third of an acre.

Oh, man. I just can't seem to stay away from this nonsense. Buh-bye peace and tranquility.

A movement to my right caught my eye. Two men! Sentries? I eased down so that my head was below the wind-blown underbrush. They were walking away from me, one in front of the other about twenty yards away. I must have barely missed happening upon them face to face.

It had been months since I used my ability to disrupt the nervous system of another human, and even longer since I had used it to take the life of a criminal. Since then, almost all of the times I had focused this energy on other living things were life or death situations involving animals. I hoped I still had a capable command of those abilities. In the middle of the woods with two armed men was probably not the best place to test that, but if I retreated and they saw me leaving, I felt sure they would not hesitate to fire at me.

I stayed hidden and watched as they made their way around the field. When the sentries made it back around, I focused on the neck of the one following the other. He collapsed and the other sentry turned around to investigate. I focused on his neck, too, and he crumpled into the coca sprouts. The first one was already beginning to recover so I refocused on his neck.

Fortunately, my skills were still sharp.

They both kept trying to reach the guns stuffed into the front of their pants, not knowing I was trying to spare their lives. I couldn't stay focused on either one of them long enough for them to lose consciousness, so I oscillated between the two while I approached. I managed to keep them both down and incapacitated while I disarmed them. The long, leather shoelace from one of their boots was handy enough to tie all four of their hands together, behind their backs.

"Shhh." A finger to my lips ensured they took my meaning.

One of them drew in a deep breath and I could tell he was going to yell for help, so I paralyzed him again, long enough for him to nearly pass out from a lack of oxygen.

"Shhhh," I repeated, wagging my finger in front of his face, being as annoying as possible. He didn't look like he was going to comply, so I tore off their sleeves and used them for gags, secured tightly around their heads with their belts.

A thorough search recovered two more firearms and two knives, which I put into my backpack. Then I made them watch me pull up all their coca plants while they wailed uncontrollably. More out of fear, it seemed, than anger.

The wind was gusting too wildly to safely burn the uprooted sprouts, and I couldn't carry them all away, so I left them. I doubted they'd live, even if someone tried to replant them.

Using one of their knives, I approached them menacingly. I pressed the sharp blade to their necks one at a time. I made it obvious to them that I could easily kill them, but I did not. Instead, I raised the blade above my head, looked at one of their chests, and jammed the blade into the ground within easy reach. Walking away, I made enough noise to sound a little reckless. When I was sure I was no longer within earshot, I circled around quietly to make sure they escaped, so I could follow them back to wherever they came from once they were free.

Cutting themselves loose took longer than I had anticipated, and one of them left with a nasty slash on his wrist. They walked to Tecuanapa, which was predictable. I could not follow them through town without raising suspicions, so I skirted around through the forest, stealthy enough to evade watchful eyes. I caught enough glimpses of the two through foliage and in between structures to follow them to their destination.

They went through the double gate of an ivy-covered fence, which was impossible to see through, and all was quiet for a few minutes. Then gunshots rang out and echoed through the small town. Toucans and other birds took flight. Dogs barked. Startled people stopped in their tracks for a brief moment, then scurried out of the streets, disappearing into homes and small businesses.

Just as the birds settled and the dogs stopped barking, the double gate swung open again and I heard the sound of several vehicles starting. A small convoy of jeeps and trucks blasted out of the gates and barreled through town.

Aw, hell. What did I do, start a turf war?

In their haste, they left the gates wide open. With all of the townspeople being huddled in their homes, I took advantage of the solitude to move closer. In the middle of the compound stood a barn-like structure with big doors on all four sides. I could see people in and behind the barn toiling away although I was still too far away to see what they were doing.

The yard between the gate and the barn was littered with supplies and trash. Some of it was in piles on the ground while other provisions were stacked on pallets. This provided ample places to hide, so I eased into the yard when no one was looking, using the supplies as cover to get closer to the barn.

From my vantage point in the supply section of the property, behind a pallet of fifty-pound bags of cement, it didn't take long to confirm that these were indeed the owners of the coca plant field. Behind the barn, several people labored under a large makeshift tent made of old tarps.

One was pouring a bag of the cement mix into a large vat, while another poured in gasoline from five-gallon cans. A woman picked up a long paddle and began stirring. When the bag of cement mix was empty, one of the guys started pouring in the contents of white, one-gallon jugs of what looked like bleach, but could have easily been sulfuric acid.

Behind the tent, the unmistakable sound of a single-stroke gas engine got my attention. I moved around the barn, still using the supplies and tree trunks as cover. A man wearing a long-sleeved shirt was running a lawnmower over a pile of leaves. A rough-looking woman raked the pieces into new piles to be mowed again.

THIS is how they manufacture cocaine? Cement, gasoline, and a lawnmower?

To my left, I noticed a young man wrestling something into a tarp he pulled from a section of the tent. I leaned back to get a better look and realized he was wrapping up the bodies of the two sentries I had encountered at the coca field.

Those two guys were likely family, or maybe neighbors, yet they were executed for allowing their crop of coca to be destroyed.

Drugs.

I wondered what I should do about this situation. Most of these people were just trying to earn money to feed themselves and their families. However, they were producing something that causes incapacitating addictions, overdoses, and children being abused or killed. Or both. Should I just try to take out the people in charge and trust that the laborers would find other jobs? Or would they go right back to producing cocaine? The people in charge might not even be local.

Tough call.

Struggling with radical choices, I watched, remaining hidden behind the bags of cement. Walk away? Kill the ones the others left behind? Or wait for everyone to return, then kill them all together? What I really wanted to do was leave and let all of this be someone else's problem, but knowing the product they were making would hurt children prevented me from abandoning this effort.

My thoughts were spinning and I ruminated far too long.

You know what? I had a little conversation with myself. *They will still be here tomorrow. I'll sleep on it.*

I took precautions on the way back to make sure I wasn't followed. Hiking through the woods towards the road to the west, I periodically stopped to scan the jungle behind me, watching for any evidence of people following me. When I was sure no one was tracking me, I headed back to camp.

Chip's Down

Chip Granberry was simply not himself since his girlfriend left without a word. Normally, he took pleasure in taking money from casinos and fellow gamblers, but this trip to Black Hawk was joyless. Some of the guys at the Texas Hold 'Em table were so easy to read, a few times he didn't even need to rely on his superior power of intuition to "see" the future.

Phil blinked a lot when he was bluffing. Don wouldn't make eye contact when he had a hand. Mark peeked at his cards more when he didn't have a decent hand and would not look at them a second time if he had a pair.

Amateurs.

His three goals for this trip were to pocket enough money to add to his investment portfolio, win an adequate amount to allow him to purposefully lose a few hands and still walk out with enough to sustain himself for two or three months. As always, he accomplished all three goals, and then he was done. Poker wasn't as fun as it used to be. Now it was just business.

He couldn't shake his lackadaisical attitude. *Whatev. Might as well head home.*

Experience had taught him to reduce risk. The time had come to lose a little money back to the amateur gamblers at the table, so they would feel sympathy for him instead of contempt. Casino eyes would also be less likely to accuse him of cheating or ban him from their establishment if they thought he was just a lucky guy who knew his luck had left him.

Chip sighed dramatically. "Well, my luck seems to be gone. That's thirteen hands in a row I've lost or folded. Cashin' out. Good luck, gentlemen."

Back in the Game

As usual, my toucan friends woke me at sunrise. They stood on their branches croaking while I sat in my treehouse contemplating life and the future.

Why am I sitting in a treehouse like a runaway adolescent? I can't do this anymore. I have to make a difference in the time I have left.

I could die any day, like those two sentries yesterday. I spared their lives but their ruthless employer shot them in the head. "They" could catch me tomorrow and either kill me or put me in prison for decades. Yes, they'd have a hard time proving I did any harm to anyone, but they might. My life was already ruined. I had nothing left to lose.

"Let's take those lowlifes out, shall we?" The toucans looked at me, but did not answer. At least not in English, as they continued croaking after a moment of silence.

The rest of the morning was spent preparing for a confrontation with a dozen people. I boiled enough water to fill the three bottles I'd saved. A walk to the beach produced two good coconuts, which I cracked open and drank. The rest would be saved for snacks while I watched the cocaine manufacturers. I wanted to figure out how I could take them all out without anyone escaping. Some mosquito netting might be useful too, in case I watched them well into the evening, so I stuffed it all in my backpack and headed back to Tecuanapa.

I climbed a tree that overlooked most of their compound and draped the mosquito netting over me, which also offered some camouflage. The front gate and the tent behind the house were in my view, but I could not see inside. No fewer than six vehicles had stormed away the previous day, but today, only two trucks remained, and one of those had shattered windows.

Their turf war did not go well for them.

Forest shadows became long and my stomach was performing convincing impersonations of a large, creaking door. Would they shut down when the sun went down? Or would they continue working? I either needed to eat my remaining coconut or get busy taking them out.

I climbed down from my tree and scaled the ivy-covered fence enough to peer over it.

When you can scramble nervous systems simply by focusing intently, killing a gang of cocaine manufacturers has virtually no risk. It probably shouldn't be so easy for me, and truthfully, it wouldn't be if innocent lives weren't at stake.

In a moment, there were dead people everywhere, and it didn't bother me a bit. I'd seen too much carnage over the years, *and* I felt as though I had ultimately saved a few lives. If only *one* child was saved, or if just a few families were spared from ruin, I felt my extreme measures were justified.

A search of the property uncovered a lot of weapons and ammo, but very little cash, all in pesos. I wasn't even disappointed. I knew what to do with the money. And I knew what to do with the truck that had no shattered windows.

If I'm back into this, I'm going to need some transportation.

The key fob was on the console, so I drove the truck down the road and stashed it behind a thick grove of bushes about a quarter of a mile away. The sun was setting by the time I walked back.

Burning product, weapons and vehicles had become routine for me. This time, there was plenty of gasoline, which made my tasks easier.

With the sun down, this fire should be spectacular. And *send a message.*

Bright orange flames leapt high into the darkness, I left the compound and walked down the middle of the town's main road. Between the flickering shadows, I could see people standing in their front doors and looking out of their windows. Their stares went back and forth between me and the blaze behind me.

If my author friend is able to make a movie out of his books about my adventures, this scene will surely make a good trailer.

I forced my face into a ridiculous, overly theatrical expression that would let the audience know how serious I was. I imagined the wild flames behind me, brilliant but out of focus, and hair I didn't have blowing in the wind.

Chuckling, I called myself a dumbass and pulled my mind back to reality.

It was difficult to know if the townspeople were angry or relieved, but I left the bag of pesos on the porch of the town store and turned to wave to the people who were still huddled in their homes. As I walked through town, one old man offered me a half nod from his doorway, which I returned, but I kept moving.

The forest was too dark and unpredictable to hike through for long. I used the flashlight feature on my phone to search for the truck I had taken from the cocaine manufacturers, but it was hard to know which path to take. I found the hidden truck, but considering the road I was on, staying put for the night seemed wise. If I drove back near my camp, I would have to hide the vehicle again, which wouldn't be easy at night and *could* be potentially dangerous.

Spending the night there sounded more appealing than wandering around at night, so I opened both windows about a quarter of an inch and settled myself into the seat with my feet propped up on the door. I attempted to use my backpack for a pillow, but it was too hard and bulky. As I tried to get comfortable, mosquitos found their way through the cracks.

Irritated, I closed the passenger-side window, opened the driver's-side door, draped my mosquito netting from my backpack around it, and then closed the door. I swatted the mosquitos that had already found their way in until all the humming was gone. Then I went back to trying to get comfortable.

I was too far away from the burning compound to see the glow of the flames, but occasionally, in the dim starlight, I could see smoke billowing through the trees. I couldn't help but wonder if the townspeople were standing there watching it all burn. For them, dawn would bring a whole new day.

Soothing sounds made their way through the dense forest. The ringing in my ears muffled much of it, I'm sure, although I could still hear wind whispering through the trees and a mottled owl hooting in the distance. Later, a soaking rain pattered the truck and the leaves. When the rain mellowed into a gentle sprinkle, the hooting began again.

Owls and I go way back. If you spend as much time as I do in forests at night, you're bound to hear a few. They always bring me comfort. The hooting stopped again, though, when the two of us heard someone laughing. I would have thought I had imagined it if the mottled owl hadn't stopped hooting. The laughter wasn't devious or maniacal, or anything like that, it was more whimsical, or even musical. It echoed through the forest, making it impossible to know from which direction it came. I must have fallen asleep listening for more.

In the morning, I stretched away the stiffness and drove to Coatzacoalcos for a smartphone. I downloaded a language translation app that did not need a phone signal or Internet connection to work.

Back in the tiny town of Tecuanapa, I returned to the home of the old man who acknowledged me with a half nod, but no one answered my knock. The little store was open, so I walked over there and, sure enough, he was behind the counter. Probably the owner.

The old man thought the translator app was the most amazing thing ever and stared at it with big eyes. After I showed him how to use it, we talked for nearly an hour about other cocaine and opiate manufacturers in the area. During that time, no one visited his store. When I asked about that, he responded through the translator. "Almost everyone is at the cemetery, burying the dead."

"Oh, right." I hadn't thought much about the aftermath of my efforts to rid the world of drug dealers and terrorists.

Wow. What kind of person am I? Maybe getting back in the game was a mistake. I seem to be changing.

He added, "They will be busy most of the day."

Lost in thought, I stared through the window at the smoke still rising from my carnage. After a few awkward moments, I asked, "Would you, and most others, prefer it if I just went away? Or would you rather I stayed long enough to take out any other drug manufacturers in the area?"

"You could do that? By yourself?"

"Sí."

As he walked out from behind the ancient cash register, he choked on a few of his own words. "One of the men they... shot, yesterday, was... was my grandson." He pulled a dusty map off one of his shelves, opened it with purpose onto the counter, and marked the areas where he suspected similar activities were occurring. I thanked him by paying for the map with a sizable roll of American dollars.

Better Bitter than Broke

Soon after Jeanna learned that her old boss was wanted by the FBI, her boyfriend urged her to get her hands on as much of her money as she could. "If the feds seize your money, you will never see it again."

When she hadn't heard from her boss in several months, she sold their business, pocketing her part, which was about three million dollars. The lawyers put her boss's cut into a trust account, in case he returned someday. But because her boss had no beneficiaries listed, if the trust fund went unclaimed for five years, the funds were to be dispersed evenly to all the employees who had lost their jobs when the business was sold.

Jeanna took her boyfriend's advice, but not fast enough. On Valentine's Day, of all days, they confiscated all the money in her ex-boss's trust fund. They would have seized her accounts, too, if Special Agent Carla Bright hadn't argued for simply freezing her accounts. The remaining million and a half was still there, but could be tied up in court for years. Jeanna was thankful she'd paid cash for her home. Her monthly expenses were minimal, so she could easily live a few years with the $220,000 she'd stashed in safe deposit boxes.

She felt like she owed her old boss *big*-time for making her a full partner in the company he had founded. He had hired her to simply manage a handful of clients, but she was the one who wrangled in so many new contracts she had to hire more employees. The new clientele created a steady flow of cash, which was what had attracted the attention of the investors who bought the company. Singlehandedly, Jeanna made that lucrative sale possible.

Still, the millions Jeanna made would not have come to fruition without her old boss. She was understandably bitter when she found out he was wanted by the FBI. It just didn't seem possible.

A serial killer? Really? He seemed so kind.

Sweet Ride

My new truck came in handy while doing reconnaissance for a few days southwest of Vigía Chico, which was the closest of the four places the old man had marked on his map. Each day, I witnessed two thugs drive into Felipe Carrillo Puerto, and then to some of the smaller towns nearby. They collected what was probably drug money from other, presumably lesser thugs, *and* took hard-earned money from angry or terrified shop owners.

I followed them to a home on the coast near Vigía Chico, which was their last stop, every day. They reported to a man who I presumed was the homeowner, giving him all the money they had collected that day. Arrogant and verbally abusive to his men, he was easy to dislike. I nicknamed him "Robbinmahood."

Robbinmahood steals from the poor to make himself rich.

He was evidently doing well. His modern, oceanfront home was made of pinewood and imported stone from Spain, all of it trimmed with beautiful, oil-stained Mexican Royal Ebony. Tall windows spanned two floors. Multiple second-story balconies overlooked the estate and a pergola in the back yard shaded posh, patio furniture. A large outdoor grill and a kitchenette provided even more living space. The home was incredible. Most houses in the area were stucco-covered cinder blocks, but this outlaw flaunted his wealth and power.

Perched atop a wooded bluff, the mini-mansion overlooked a quiet cove on the Yucatan peninsula and featured an elaborate, multitier pool in the back. There was a private dock and plenty of space between neighbors. Several expensive cars and SUVs were permanent fixtures in the front because there was only a two-car garage. Robbinmahood had an entourage of bodyguards and cronies who parked their vehicles in the yard, on what was once a nice lawn. Unfortunately, the home also had an exhaustive security system.

They don't deserve to live so well. I don't either, really, but I'm taking this Thug House anyway, to make it my new home base.

Because of the security system, the power to the house would need to be cut if I was going to get in and take over. But if I cut the electricity to the house by damaging wires or switches, I'd have a hard time getting someone out to restore the power. I knew I would need to disrupt the electricity in the entire area. It's easier than most people realize, and if you use magnets and plenty of metal shavings, there's no damage to the equipment at all. It just takes a few hours to find the problem and clean it up.

A hardware store in Felipe Carrillo Puerto provided powerful, construction cleanup magnets. Steel wool that wasn't covered in soap and an entire box of steel washers would double as metal shavings. I also picked up heavy-duty bolt cutters to get into the subdivision transformer, and a thick pair of work gloves.

Later that night, a bright, gibbous moon provided enough light to put my plan into motion. Although cutting through the industrial grade padlock was a laborious effort, the heavy bolt cutters did the trick. I lifted the half-lid top of the transformer up and over, so it rested on the other side. Filling that panel with the shredded steel wool and washers, I strategically placed magnets on the inside so they would catch most of the fragments when the panel slammed shut. When it came time to close the transformer though, I was somewhat apprehensive.

Is this thing going to blow up or throw sparks?

I still had the rest of the twine I used for my treehouse, so I pulled it out of my backpack and tied one end to the panel of the transformer. While rolling it out, I got to the end a lot sooner than I had hoped. I was not pleased with how little was left. Eighteen to twenty feet would have to do.

Crouching down to make myself a smaller target for sparks and debris, I positioned myself in a way that gave me the leverage I might need to pull the heavy panel back into place, but was also flight-friendly, in case I needed to make a run for it.

Okay, let's do this.

Squinting, I pulled the string. A little harder. I clenched my teeth, and other things, and gave it a good tug. The panel swung over and slammed shut with a solid thud as I threw myself to the ground, expecting the worst. I heard some tinkling from the steel washers and a short, loud hum as all the lights to my right went out. There were no explosions. There weren't even any sparks. My plan to take out the power in the area simply worked.

I unclenched everything, rolled over onto my back, had a good laugh, then jumped up and hurried back to Robinmahood's house.

Apparently, when the power went out, the justifiably-paranoid homeowner had sent all six of his underlings outside to place themselves into defensive positions around the house. This just made it easy to take them out. I walked up the long driveway, waving like I was a neighbor with questions about the power outage situation. I dropped all six of the thugs so quickly that Robbinmahood didn't know there was a problem until I confronted him in his own living room. He was on his mobile phone, probably trying to get the electricity back on.

I forced him to empty all the pockets of the dead, and pile their bodies into the back of the largest of his SUVs. Getting him to open his huge safe took a lot more *persuading*. The reasons for his dogged resistance became clear after the heavy door finally swung open. That safe contained stacks upon stacks of American money, mostly one-hundred-dollar bills. Jackpot! There were a lot of pesos, too, which I didn't even bother to count. Some gaudy men's jewelry and several pieces of small but exquisite Mayan relics added an unknown value to the mix.

All that was for later. The most pressing task at the moment was to dispose of the bodies, including the homeowner, before sunrise.

Talking to Robbinmahood like we were old buddies, I made a suggestion. "Let's take that SUV to a secluded spot in Sian Ka'an, shall we? You drive."

"Why would I help you, *pendejo*?"

"To live, of course. Drive, or I'll drop you where you stand."

His face compressed into an expression of contempt, but he complied and drove to Sian Ka'an with me riding shotgun. He pulled off the road behind a grove of trees and turned off the lights.

"Well? What are you waiting for? Drag the bodies out of the back."

Using the flashlight feature on his phone, I watched him closely, and as I suspected, he tried to run after he dumped the first body. I focused on his legs and watched him tumble into the jumble of tall grass and sticks. A long string of Spanish obscenities only stopped after I walked over and focused on his neck.

"Do you want to die here, or do you want me to drop you off in Campeche?"

Calming down at the thought of surviving the ordeal, the abuser of families and killer of children cooperated fully. He dragged the bodies out, one by one. When he finished, he stood over them and looked sad.

"You know, *pendejo*, one of these men was mi primo. We grew up together."

"Well then, I think it would only be fair if you rotted together, too."

"Bah! You said you would drop me off in Campeche!"

"Yeah. Well," I sighed indifferently while scratching the back of my neck. "I wanted you to feel hope for a moment, and then fully experience hope being crushed, much like that of your victims."

Another string of Spanish curse words was again cut short, permanently this time, as I killed him and watched him fall across two of the other bodies. I wondered if one of them was his cousin.

Robbinmahood knew the risks involved in illegal drug trafficking, and the consequences.

The fool's pockets did not contain anything the police might trace back to my new house, so I covered the bodies with grass, leaves and sticks.

A soothing orange sunrise woke me after a couple of hours of deep sleep. I looked around at first, wondering whose comfy couch I was on. The next thing that attracted my attention were dramatic, east-facing, floor-to-ceiling windows designed to allow the warm colors of the sunrise to fill the room. As I watched, the sun peeked majestically over the Caribbean Sea. Shimmering reflections danced across the waves all the way to the horizon.

Wow. What a view.

I found the coffee machine but the electricity was still off, so I explored my new place, which was extensive. And beautiful. None of the wood was painted. It was all sanded to a soft touch and stained. I wasn't a fan of all the walls being gray, but the furniture was also wood, covered in leather where appropriate, and solid. From the rooftop deck I noticed the white top of my new boat, swaying with the waves.

Oh, I have to go check that out.

Hanging by the back door were several sets of keys, only one of which was attached to a float. I took the stairs behind the house. As I weaved down a flagstone path through a thick forest of trees, the boat came into view.

"Oh, no. No, no, no. Seriously?" I exclaimed aloud as I immediately recognized the type of boat. It was a late forties or early fifties, all-wood, Chris-Craft Deluxe Enclosed. To no one, I yelled, "SWEET!" It looked to be about thirty feet long and had been restored recently. As the name suggests, it had an enclosed cabin with a tiny kitchenette, a toilet, and down below the bow deck it slept four "comfortably" on two sets of bunk beds.

These bad boys sell for a hundred thousand dollars or more. I love a Chris-Craft.

Her straight six fired right up, purring like an overgrown cat. The gas tank was over half full and the weather looked calm, so I took her out for a ride. She went from idle to planed-out in only four or five seconds, while the heavy craft took two-foot Caribbean Sea waves with hardly a jolt. What a ride!

A Campfire in the Sand

There was so much money in the safe that it took all day just to count the American bills. Over seven million dollars, which I found difficult to leave in the safe. All that idle cash was driving me nuts. At least *some* of it could be earning interest or dividends, although finding ways to invest would prove to be a challenge. Opening a bank account in my own name would raise red flags, so I needed to find a way around that.

I thought back over the aliases I had used in the past and remembered the Steven Andrews identification I had set up. The feds had found his driver's license and other info, I'm sure, and had seized assets and all the money I left in the bank account for bills, but were they still watching that alias?

Only one way to find out.

An old email in the Drafts folder contained all of Steven's information, so I bought a new burner smartphone to use exclusively for this endeavor. While sitting on a Caribbean Sea beach, I created an account with an online financial institution. A bank in Felipe Carrillo Puerto let me purchase cashier's checks with American dollars, so I started with $50,000. I mailed the check to the new bank account and in ten business days the deposit showed up. I notified the IRS by making an estimated tax payment to avoid the $10K+ flag being an issue. I reported the money as Foreign Income.

Since no one seized the money or locked the account, I assumed I was good to go for the time being. With nothing to lose, I made some solid investments like CDs and a few ETFs, but knowing there was no risk involved in spending someone else's money, I also invested in a couple of the cryptocurrency technologies.

Made me feel better.

Getting back to business, my next target was in the Chacah area off the shores of Laguna de Términos. The area on the map the old man in Tecuanapa had circled was relatively close to shore. I could easily take my new Chris-Craft around the Yucatan peninsula, and gain access via the lagoon.

Not wanting to put it off, I loaded up the boat with a week's supply of food, water and pesos. I opened all the windows in the cab and shoved off. Engine purring. Warm wind in my hair. Cruising in style. I enjoyed waving at other boaters who also loved my old, luxury Chris-Craft. As free as one can be.

I had to slow down to watch a pod of dolphins skipping over the waves in front of me. They seemed to join me for a short while, but then headed off on their own.

It wasn't long before I needed gas, so I pulled into the first marina I could find. The tank was not quite empty, but it only took twenty-eight gallons to fill it. I could easily run out of gas between marinas, so I purchased two five-gallon gas cans and filled them up. Fortunately, there were marinas all along the gulf coast. Unfortunately, I was only averaging about thirty-two miles per hour.

The vintage work of art was meant more for cruising around a lake than it was for long ocean hauls, but I forged on in style. When it was too dark to go on, I anchored off the northwest tip of the Yucatan peninsula. Fresh ocean air soothed me to my core, while gentle waves rocked me into a sound sleep. The trip took over a day and a half, but the coastline was beautiful and the freedom refreshing.

Laguna de Términos has some of the most stunning beaches and coastline I've ever seen. In many places, palm trees grew out and over the waves, stretching out twenty-five or thirty feet.

I found a clear spot between palm groves large enough to beach my Chris-Craft, yet hidden from prying eyes on land. The craft slid up onto the inconspicuous beach and came to a firm rest in the sand, but I dropped the anchor too, in case high tide came in. The GPS on the boat told me I was close to my target. All I needed to do was walk southeast through thick, untamed forests and swamps full of bloodthirsty insects and caiman, look for suspicious activity, confirm that they really are cocaine-producing criminals, and take them out.

That's all.

Fighting my way through the thick foliage was far more time consuming than I had anticipated. I hiked for hours, but eventually, a beautiful orange horizon drove me back to my boat.

Wish I had a state-of-the-art drone.

Morning was better. The old man in Tecuanapa was correct, although the camp was on the extreme southern edge of his circle, far from my boat. I watched the cocaine factory for a while to get an idea of their comings and goings. At one point, a big, black SUV full of rough-looking people showed up.

Now is my time.

I moved a little closer and swept a sharp focus through their camp and factory. People folded over and fell to the ground. Except for one guy who looked around, shrieked, and ran. I focused on him specifically, and when I was sure he was dead, I swept the entire area again.

As far as spoils go, Laguna de Términos was a bust. I only found about twelve thousand in U.S. dollars and another hundred and fifty thousand in pesos. I burned all their product, structures, equipment, vehicles, and weapons. No one would ever use these facilities again.

When I got back to my boat, I had some surprises waiting for me. Low tide had it sitting completely on the beach, and that wasn't the worst of it. There must have been fifteen spider monkeys climbing all over my beautiful Chris-Craft, screeching and screaming. I wasn't going anywhere.

Laguna de Términos translates to The Lagoon of Ends. Meaning the area is where several rivers and streams end. *That* meant fresh water was abundant in the area. Where mosquitos live and breed. Millions of them. Maybe billions.

If I can't get into the cabin before sundown, I will be eaten alive.

Highly motivated, a campfire soon blazed on the sand, away from the piles of driftwood and dry underbrush where the jungle met the beach. As the fire began to grow, the monkeys became more and more vocal. They jumped up and down, screaming and hugging each other. Some were looking at me and my fire, while others also looked into the foliage with equal hysteria.

Okay, good. Their natural habitat is looking better and better to them.

The monkeys looked back and forth at me and the forest as I approached the boat with two flaming branches. They were becoming so stressed I felt sure they would attack, but they did not. The intensity of their fits continued to escalate.

Wait, they are not looking at the forest as a place where they might escape, they are looking at something in *the forest.*

I followed their fearful glances but couldn't see anything except foliage. I moved around the boat and placed myself between the monkeys and the general area of their attention, and they calmed down a bit. Waving the flaming branches around, I moved closer to the dense underbrush... until I locked eyes with a jaguar.

I froze. Poised in the foliage, not twelve feet away, the cat was waiting for the right moment to pounce. My hair stood on end. The size of the beast surprised me.

The jaguar knew it had been spotted and snarled an unmistakable warning as it moved into an attack posture. I put one burning branch directly into the gaze of the beautiful but terrifying creature, and waved the other over my head.

Am I going to have time to react before this cat rips me some new ones?

Our standoff didn't last long. The cat's apprehension and caution prevailed. It turned and retreated into the woods. Behind me, the raucous grew to a new crescendo. This time, the clamor had a different sound. Definitely more relief than stress. They hugged and jumped up and down. Still in my boat.

I was relieved too, but backed away from the woods, continuing to wave the burning branches. When I kicked sand over the fire and the smoke dwindled and stopped, the spider monkeys calmed down. One of them finally jumped out of my boat and the others followed. As a group, they scampered up the beach and took to the trees.

Although my boat was trashed, it was not nearly the mess I thought it would be, so I went straight to the cabin, shut the door behind me, and closed all the windows.

I'll deal with the clutter in the morning. I just hope this cabin is tight enough to keep the mosquitos out.

To the Cenotes

When I woke, the tide was up and there were no monkeys on my boat. My mind was fresh and my eyes were bright. I heaved the anchor in and headed back to my new home in Vigía Chico. On the way, I decided that getting around in a vintage Chris-Craft might be the absolute coolest way to travel, but I needed to be able to get from point A to point B faster.

One more peaceful night on the ocean and another in my new home with no jaguars, monkeys or mosquitos had me wondering if I wanted to continue living the life of a vigilante. Every time I played the part of a stranger in a strange land, I always seemed to get into dangerous situations, or at least regretted being extremely uncomfortable.

I could just retire and enjoy my life here in this mini-paradise. Let the cocaine manufacturers continue to pump drugs into America to feed the addictions they helped establish.

Then I recalled why I always get involved. Innocent children. How many kids have to die so that people can get high? I shook off the Quitter's Blues and drove a luxury SUV to the area southeast of Reserva Estatal Geohidrológica Anillo de Cenotes.

Three long days of reconnaissance in the thick jungle found no evidence of illegal activity or substances, but I was astounded that I had never seen nor understood what a cenote was. Who would have thought that a big sinkhole partially filled with water could be so magnificently beautiful and fascinating? They were all different in many unique ways, each having its own unique ecosystem.

Ferns, elephant ears, hummingbirds and frogs were commonplace. Intricate, delicate spider webs protected from the wind glistened in the noon sunlight. Trees overhung the ponds far below and colorful, singing birds perched on them, waiting for their next meal to fly by or crawl too close. The chorus of birdsong echoed around inside the cenote, amplifying and dispersing it into an orchestra far superior to any high-tech surround-sound system.

Stunning.

Tourists were visiting, too. A lot of tourists. Mostly on guided tours. I snagged a map of the reserve from one of the guides and reasoned that any illegal activity would be away from the "ring of cenotes" and all the tourists.

Backpacking through the Yucatan jungle was interesting. It was not like my peaceful hike through Canada at all. For one thing, the leeches were bad. I had learned to keep a roll of duct tape in my backpack for emergency repairs, and to help keep insects and leeches off my skin. Using the tape to close off sleeves and pants legs kept most of them off, but I'll admit that I'd rather camp with bears than leeches. Fires discourage most bears, but the heat campfires generate often attracts more leeches than is deterred, so I hiked back to my SUV every evening.

On my fourth day of reconnaissance, while walking north from a fork in a dirt road about a mile to a mile and a half northwest of Chichi, I heard a single gunshot. I stopped and squatted, but when I heard a woman sobbing uncontrollably, I made my way in her direction as quietly as possible. The persistent ringing in my ears made it hard to pinpoint where the crying was coming from, but I kept searching until I found her.

A man-made clearing in the jungle hid four small grass huts and one larger shelter sturdier than the others. The woman's haunting, mournful cry came from within one of the pitiful huts. The tone of her crying had changed from hysteria to something that might have been resignation, but she was far from getting back in control of herself.

I could not see inside any of the shelters, but as I moved around to get a better look, I saw the likely reason the poor woman was crying. A man was face down in a puddle of what looked like his own blood and brain matter. His hands were tied behind his back and a rope that had probably once bound his legs together was still wrapped around one ankle.

What the hell? It might take a little while to figure out what is going on here, but as long as there is a woman crying in a hut in the middle of the jungle, I can't just leave.

Wary of the ruthlessness of someone willing to shoot a helpless and bound individual in the back of the head, and ignoring a crying woman in a hut, I hid and watched. I settled in, expecting to be waiting a long time.

Before an hour passed, a small pickup showed up. The truck stopped in the jungle a few yards before entering the clearing. Two men with automatic weapons slung over their shoulders exited the larger shelter and two more men got out of the pickup. They spoke briefly, then one of the armed men walked with purpose to the hut containing the woman and entered. She screamed again and demanded that he tell her what he was doing, but the man was silent. A few moments later he pulled her out of the hut by her hair.

Oh, I'm killing him, for sure.

She followed him head first to minimize the pain of being led by a handful of hair, but because she wasn't fighting or resisting, the screaming almost seemed obligatory.

He forced her face in front of his and yelled. "Your husband missed the deadline, too! Do you want to end up like the good Dr. Cooper?" With that, he used the handful of hair to move her head within inches of the dead man's head wound. The screaming escalated into full hysteria again. The gaping hole in his head must have been too much for her. He repeatedly slapped her head and face with his free hand until she was quiet.

Move away from her just a little you son of a bitch. I dared not focus on his mind for fear of hurting her, too.

"Where is your husband?"

"I don't know! How would I know?"

"Is he coming? Or are you not worth the *dinero* it will cost him to get you back?"

Freaking kidnappers.

She was terrified, but she managed to sputter a response. "Two hundred and fifty thousand dollars in cash is not easy to get! Most of our money is tied up in IRAs and 401Ks. He can't just make a withdrawal at an ATM."

"Is that right?" He smacked her again, apparently just because he wanted to. "You doctors take a lot of money from the sick and *desesperado*. We both know you have *mucho dinero*."

"Again, I'm not that kind of doctor."

"Still, he will find the *dinero* somewhere, or you will wind up like your *amigo* here."

With that, he waved the two unarmed men over to join him. "If the husband shows up or calls, tell him it's now *three* hundred thousand, and take this *basura* with you." He kicked the lifeless body of the doctor and pulled the woman back to her hut by her hair while the other two began dragging the body to their truck. He stayed in the hut with the hostage so long that I feared he was doing more than just tying her up.

Should I intervene now, or wait for a better moment?

She wasn't screaming again, so I waited. The two men who had driven to the clearing were about to lift the body of Dr. Cooper into the bed of their truck when the armed man who had remained silent turned and walked back towards the larger structure. I decided I couldn't wait and took the three of them out. I continued to wait for the fourth man, still hoping that all he was doing in there was tying her up.

Come UP with a Plan?

Al picked up the phone on the first ring. "Kemal."

An Eastern Europe accent speaking English almost got Al's attention.

"Detective Alparslan Kemal?"

"Yes. Turkish Special Investigator. To whom am I speaking?" Al continued working on yesterday's paperwork.

"That's not important. I have a tip for you, if you're interested."

Almost interested enough to pay attention, Al let an irritated "Yes?" escape his lips.

"I arrived in Klaipėda, Lithuania yesterday and met with a young, cocky Asian man who tried to hire me to hack American servers."

"Uh huh."

The voice on the phone added, "Government and corporate servers."

"Okay, out of all the more appropriate law enforcement agencies available to report this incident, you chose to call me specifically. Why?" Al signed his name with a flourish, closed the file he was working on, placed it in the Out box, and opened the next file.

The man on the phone sounded a little irritated. "This is the point where you stop multitasking and listen."

Sighing and leaning back in his chair, the investigator summoned enough patience to keep from barking at the man. "Sorry. I'm all yours."

"It's not *what* he was doing that will interest you, but *who*. It was someone that I think you are looking for, who goes by the name of Qian."

Al lunged forward, knocking a few things off his cluttered desk. "Who is this?"

"You, too, were working undercover for years, so when I say I can't tell you, you'll understand. What I *can* tell you is where he will be this weekend. Can you meet me here in Klaipėda tomorrow?"

"I can try, but *where* in Klaipėda? Big town."

"Meet me outside the Lithuanian Sea Museum. You'll have to take the Old Ferry to the Curonian Spit."

With a dubious expression, Al guessed at the spelling. "When, and, how will I know you?"

"I'll be near the oldest fishing ship in the section called The Grounds of Old Fishing Ships. When the sun sets, I will leave. If you're not there, we've missed our chance."

Still scribbling, Al asked, "The Grounds of, what?"

"The Grounds of Old Fishing Ships. You can't miss it. They are beautiful old boats."

"I will be there if it is possible, but you're already there. Why can't you arrest him?"

The man on the phone tried to contain his irritation, but was not entirely successful. "Because my cover would be compromised! This guy Qian is not our target. The jackals he is trying to do business with are our targets. I'll finish briefing you in person, and we can come up with a plan, but for now, I must go."

"Wait! *'Come UP with a plan'*?"

No response.

"Hello? Are you there?" Another sigh accompanied dialing his C.O.'s extension. While the phone rang, he wondered if his boss would be yelling or screaming today.

"What?"

Yelling.

"I need to go to Klaipėda, Lithuania, right now."

"No, you don't! Who the hell do you think you are?"

Struggling to maintain enough control to keep from yelling back, Al simply said, "I have a lead on Qian."

"GET OFF THE PHONE AND GO!" Click.

And screaming.

One last sigh.

Ds and Fs

As soon as he stepped out of the hut and away from her, I killed him as dead as I could make him. The poor, stressed-out woman became hysterical again when her captor collapsed, so I waited for her to not only calm down, but to see if anyone else would exit the shelter.

Rather than calm down, she began yelling for help, which probably meant there was no one else left in the shelter. I approached the hut with caution.

"Please help me. Please! PLEASE get me out of here."

I suppressed smartass retorts about what a good idea she had and how the thought hadn't yet occurred to me. "Is anyone else here?"

"I don't know. That guy just fell down a minute ago, but I don't think he's dead."

In the center of her hut was a tree trunk about five feet high that the hut was built around. Her back was against the trunk and her arms were stretched around behind it with her wrists tied together.

"Let's get out of here, then." I whipped out my pocket knife to cut her loose and she screamed again. "Oh, geez, just calm down, okay?"

"Yes, sorry. You have no idea what I've been through."

"No doubt." I carefully cut her wrists free. "What's your name?"

"Carol. Why?"

I ignored her question and the fact that she didn't ask me for my name. "Carol, can you drive that pickup?"

"I don't know, but I bet the other hostage can."

"Right." I started to ask why she didn't mention the other hostage when I asked if anyone else was there just seconds earlier, but let it go and began cutting the bonds around her ankles. "Okay, I know this will be unpleasant for you, but I need you to check all five bodies for mobile phones and money."

Her face contorted into a mixture of horror and repugnance.

"Do it *now*. We have to get out of here."

"Okay," she snapped, and hurried away.

This poor woman is a mess.

The guy in the other hut was tied more securely and gagged. Both eyes were blackened, his upper lip was swollen on the left side, and dried blood was caked under his nose. He gasped for air when I removed his gag.

Between breaths, he whispered, "Thank you, friend, thank you! I will never be able to repay you for this, for as long as I live."

As I cut through his bindings, I mindlessly assured him that he could. "Oh! You can repay me, no worries. Just donate money to community colleges every year and we'll call it even."

"What?"

"Seriously. That's not so bad, right?" I continued to cut through the excessive layers of ropes they had around him.

"Wha... how much money?"

"I don't know, enough to make a difference, but don't go broke. What's your name?" I was still struggling with the nylon rope around his arms and chest.

"Bill."

The woman rushed up and squatted in the entrance to the hut, her state of mind swinging from hysteria to exuberance with her news.

"One of them had all this money, and two of them had phones!" She had a wad of bills in one hand, both phones in the other, and was trying to hand it all to me.

"Bill, I assume you've met Carol. You two will need to hang on to all that cash. You're going to need it for gas and bribes to get out of this area, or you'll wind up kidnapped again. Take that pickup and head to Mérida. Contact law enforcement there, but understand, you may have to bribe them."

"What? Really?" She genuinely could not believe that law enforcement could be bribed.

The guy moaned when his restraints finally fell away. He looked like he was trying to massage his arms, but could not. All his extremities were numb from lack of circulation.

"Yes. Do *not* trust local authorities. Most of them are good, decent people, but some are not. Ransoming rich people is a big, booming business in Mexico." I made air quotes around the word "rich."

She saw her fellow hostage's discomfort and stepped in to help by massaging his arms. The circulation was returning and causing him some distress. We both helped him out of the hut so he could stand and stretch.

I had two bottled waters and three energy bars left in my backpack and gladly gave it all to them. I had more supplies in the SUV, so I wasn't worried.

She queried me while they downed the water. "Who are you? What's your name? We have to repay you somehow."

Glancing at Bill to remind him of what I had said earlier, I turned to her and made a suggestion. "You can repay me by telling the authorities that your captors caught a fever and died, and you two escaped, *but*, leave me *out* of your stories."

"Oh, it's like that, is it? They were cutting in on your profits, weren't they?" Poor Carol's mind was all over the place. The guy and I looked at each other again, knowing we were both thinking something similar like, *no wonder the guy didn't pay the ransom.* Fortunately, we both kept our petty thoughts to ourselves.

"Uhhh, no. Nothing like that. If you *must* know, I'm trying to track down and destroy cocaine facilities."

"Oh. Sorry."

I had to laugh a little but I also needed to distract them from the current conversation, so I helped the guy get to the pickup. On the way, he asked, "Hey, how'd you kill those fellas, anyway?"

With another redirect in mind, I put on a serious expression, leaned in, and with a lowered voice said, "With one of the Pentagon's new toys, but remember, for the rest of your lives, those 'fellas' must have died from a fever, and you escaped on your own."

"What about the other hostage they killed? We can't just leave him here."

He was right about that.

We wrapped the body in a thin blanket from my backpack and eased it into the bed of the pickup.

"Park near a police station, dial 911 on one of the phones, describe the pickup and tell them to look in the back. Wipe that phone clean and leave it with the pickup, and then get away as fast as you can. When you're a few blocks away, call a cab with the other phone."

Then they were gone. I searched the huts but found nothing of value, so I gathered their weapons and headed back to my SUV. On the way, I threw the weapons into a tight ravine and covered them with dirt, rocks and leaves.

Back where I left my SUV I found nothing but broken glass on the ground.

Ds! And! Fs! I was counting *on that water.*

Ants and Undies

In the middle of freaking nowhere.

If I hurried, I might be able to catch one of those tourist buses. Most of them were probably based in Mérida. Taking off at a trot, I retraced my steps back to the cenotes. The driver didn't ask for money or even seem to notice me at all. I climbed on the bus like I belonged there, without asking for permission or offering any information. From Mérida, I caught another bus back to Vigía Chico and walked back to the house from there.

In the morning, I picked the oldest of the remaining four vehicles, hoping it would be a little less likely to be stolen. The fourth area that the old man in Tecuanapa had circled was north of Nuevo Put, which is a town so small and remote that it is not even on a lot of maps.

The area the old man had suggested was only a couple of miles from the dirt road, but it was thick jungle. Sweat sprayed every time my machete encountered a vine or limb, splattering drops on the heavy foliage around me. I felt like Jack in the movie *Romancing the Stone*, cutting his way through the rainforest. Only it wasn't raining, it was my sweat. Quite the cardio workout.

Spider monkeys shrieked loud complaints while they threw sticks and unripe fruit at me. I tried to ignore them, but they didn't like that either. Talking to them calmly had no effect, and they seemed particularly offended when I sang to them. I admit they weren't entirely to blame for that. The troop eventually disappeared without a farewell or a departing piece of fruit. Or at least they didn't say goodbye in English.

When they were gone, the jungle became oddly quiet and spooky. The ringing in my ears was minimal at the moment, but I couldn't hear a single bird, or even an insect. The soft squishes of my footsteps on the moist forest floor were the only sound I could hear.

Odd.

Despite the complete lack of sound, I was *sure* the jungle was sending a message. It was probably letting me know something, loud and clear, the way it did with the monkeys and birds. I was simply too unfamiliar with the environment to hear it.

I kept moving, wondering where I would be right now if I had minded my own business when I first realized I had this special ability almost four years ago. As I considered that notion, a sudden and intense burning sensation on my left calf forced a loud yelp from my throat. I stuffed the machete under my belt to investigate, but before I could pull my pant leg up, several more stings burned through my skin.

Yelling and shouting as though that would help put out nonexistent flames, I realized why they call them fire ants. And I was standing in a sea of them! My other leg burst into flames, too. Several of them had found their way under my taped pants legs to find bare skin.

For a moment I debated whether or not I should try to focus on their little brains to see if I could kill them, but remembered the effect it had on the scorpions last year. Instead of harming them, my efforts had noticeably agitated them and made them more aggressive. There were only four or five scorpions back then, but now, *thousands* of ants had me surrounded. Maybe even hundreds of thousands.

I swatted my calves and shins furiously, killing as many as I could, but the survivors kept stinging me. I danced, slapped with both hands, and tried to find a place where the ground was not moving. The stings were getting higher up my leg. If I didn't stop them immediately… well, I was no Navy SEAL. The nanosecond I found a patch of ground with no ants, off came the boots, pants and socks.

Glad I'm wearing underwear.

Using my hands to scrape them off was a mistake. Within seconds, my hands were searing, as well. Making matters worse, my yelling must have disturbed the troop of spider monkeys again, who came back to investigate. They hollered and threw things at me. I think one of them tried to urinate on me, but I was too frantic to pay attention to any of them.

The back of my machete worked wonders. I scraped them off my skin and wiped them on a branch of ivy. Fast. I scraped and scraped. They kept stinging. The burning was easily the equal of the scorpion sting last year, except now both legs and both hands boiled furiously as their solenopsin deposits attacked my cells and killed bits of tissue.

Finally, when the ants were gone, I searched my backpack for something that might help soothe insect bites or stings, but found nothing. Not even hydrocortisone. I looked around for anything that resembled aloe vera while I slammed down two bottles of water. The water didn't help much. I remained thirsty, and didn't see any aloe.

The spider monkeys continued to harass me, inching their way closer and closer.

Wait. I'm in Mexico. The spider monkeys centimetered *their way closer.*

Okay, I may be delirious.

My pants, boots and socks still swarmed with ants. I tried scraping them away with my machete and a stick, but they were stubborn, and entrenched. I had another pair of pants in my backpack, but I needed those boots. Going barefoot in the rainforests of the Yucatan would be a mistake, and possibly a fatal one.

Maybe I can smoke them out.

I always tried to keep a lighter with me, but of course, it was in my pants pocket. I had a box of matches in my backpack, so I used those instead of risking getting stung again while trying to retrieve my lighter.

Starting a campfire in a rainforest is always difficult. Finding anything dry enough to burn is challenging, but not having shoes made it close to impossible. A dead tree nearby saved me. With only six matches remaining in the box, I finally had a sustained flame. I immediately put green wood into the flame so it would both dry out enough to burn and produce the heavy smoke I needed.

Fortunately, the spider monkeys hated the fire and smoke. They moved on to something less stressful.

A tripod of forked branches strategically placed in the path of the drifting smoke worked for my boots and socks. The ants began dropping off, so I moved enough of the burning embers directly under the tripod to prevent any of them from going back to their colony for reinforcements.

I then turned my attention to my blue jeans. They were still swarming all over them, inside and out, almost unnaturally.

Hmm. I have ants in my pants.

A thick line of fire ants leading off in the direction where I encountered them disturbed me. Sure enough, a closer inspection revealed that they were going in both directions, and they were carrying pieces of my jeans back to their nest!

They're eating them? Seriously?

My pants were a hopeless case. I used my machete and some sticks to empty the pockets of my poor old jeans, which was not easy with the constant distraction of the ant stings all over my hands and legs. I tossed my pants into the fire to kill as many of them as I could. I liked my cargo pants better anyway, and this time I wrapped the duct tape even tighter around my cuffs.

But then I started slapping mosquitos on my neck, arms and hands. The jungle kind of sucks. It was getting late and I already had the fire going, which was no easy task in such a damp environment. The mosquito netting was also rolled up into an inside pocket of my backpack.

Might as well camp here for the night.

I piled enough branches on the fire to, hopefully, keep it going all night, but did not have enough dry firewood to build my usual three fires. There wasn't room for three fires, anyway.

Ants won't crawl through ash, or at least not far, so I used a piece of bark to scatter embers and ashes from the campfire in a big circle. Inside my pest-free ring, I propped my tripod branches in a wide stance to hold up my mosquito netting into a makeshift tent, including a floor. I fought several mosquitos out of my netting, curled up, and used my backpack for a pillow, but it was hard to sleep with my hands and legs still burning.

Come Up with a Plan

Detective Kemal approached an old fishing ship bathed in evening sunlight. Sitting on a bench near the ship was a disheveled man with his eyes glued to his phone. He was pecking away at an email or something. Al stood on the side of the ship that blocked the cool breeze and did his best to appear to be admiring the old, wooden craft.

Barely audible and without looking up from his phone, the man asked, "Detective Kemal, I presume?" But his accent was British, not Eastern European.

With apprehension levels soaring, Al needed to know who else knew he was here, "Yes. And you are?"

"Ah. Yes, of course." The man's accent changed to Eastern European, effectively answering Al's question. "Sit down and let's come up with a plan."

"I am here in an undercover capacity. I have no badge, weapons or cuffs."

"Don't worry. I will provide you with everything you need to arrest or kill Qian." The informant glanced in the direction of the parking lot.

"Thank you." Al appreciated that. "Let's get straight to it. Where is he?"

"He will be in a loud, obnoxious bar later this evening. We should get there before he arrives, so we can familiarize ourselves with the layout."

"Agreed." Al kept his responses short and hoped this Brit would do the same.

"We should arrive separately, but when we get there, you watch me. I'll be talking to several people. If I am standing when I speak to him, I'll put one thumb in my pocket, like this." He demonstrated needlessly. "If I am sitting, then I will cross my arms on the table like this." He held his arms out, one atop the other.

"Oh, I will recognize him when I see him." The memory of Qian was forever etched into Al's memory. When he and Carla had encountered him in Turkmenistan, they did not realize he was a wanted man. By the time they learned who he was, he had already slipped away.

"Maybe. He is known for being able to change his appearance drastically."

"Got it."

Back in his native British accent, and more somber, the man offered some sage advice. "Kemal, do not hesitate to pull the gun I'll give you and kill that bloody criminal on the spot. Knowing where Qian is going to be is a rare occurrence indeed. If we fail tonight, countless others are sure to suffer or die."

On the Trail Again

Morning was hard. Instead of sunlight, there was a gray glow. A light rain woke me. My joints ached after lying on the damp ground of the forest, and I cringed as my pants scraped the swollen blisters over each ant sting. Powering through the pain would be difficult, but I was not about to let it slow me down. It was simply something I had to endure to finish my task.

Breaking camp was easy. The rain put out my campfire and there was no tent to take down and stow. All I had to do was shake the water from my netting as best as I could while I rolled it up, and then I was on my way. I paid more attention to the ground this time. I always watched for snakes, but I also needed to keep an eye out for anything resembling an ant hill.

I hiked most of the day, with the first half being in a light drizzle that still soaked me. I finally noticed a hint of a dirt road that was more of a mud road at the moment. It didn't appear to have been used recently, or often, but the wide path was unmistakable. I followed it deeper into the jungle, and sure enough, found a mature coca field.

A slow, but complete circumnavigation around the large field, through mud and thick rainforest foliage, found no sign of guards or caretakers. Camping overnight again would save me a return trip in the morning, so I built my three campfires far enough from the field and the dirt road to avoid being seen, and settled into a cozier campsite than the previous night. The forest was thick and a string of small waterfalls in a stream helped conceal any noise I made. Each waterfall splashed into pools of varying sizes that stepped down a long, gentle slope.

Beautiful campsite. I took pictures of the waterfalls while I retrieved a panful of water, and while that boiled, I gathered more firewood. Settling in for the night, I enjoyed the peaceful sunset from the center of my campfires.

Learned a lesson. Don't camp on the ground near fresh water in an equatorial rainforest.

A grunting growl woke me from a light sleep. Whatever the animal was, it sounded big.

Seriously? Man, I just can't catch a break.

I was glad I had spent the extra time to build three fires, but the thing about being surrounded by fires is that it's difficult to see past them. The darkness beyond the flames becomes infinite, and whatever lurks beyond the blaze remains hidden. All you can do is throw on more wood to build your fires up enough to frighten off the predators.

Getting out from under my mosquito netting introduced another problem. Instantly, insects swarmed around my body and began chewing me to bits. I picked up the cool end of a burning branch and waved it around, hoping to deter the bugs. Didn't help much.

Meanwhile, whatever was stalking me was large enough to not care about the noises it made circling me, looking for a way around the fires and into my camp. I peered through the darkness, first squinting, then opening my eyes wide, but I could not see the beast. Finally, I realized I was looking in the wrong direction. I had assumed it was another jaguar or other large cat, but I spotted two pairs of glowing eyes low to the ground. Caimans!

I hurled the burning branch at them, but it fell short. Sparks flew and reptilian tempers flared, but they did not back down. They stopped moving and advancing, but the glowing eyes stayed put. I placed more green wood on the campfires and found other medium-sized, burning branches to toss at them. Finally, a hot ember landed directly on one of the caimans. Making a big fuss and then huffing their displeasure, they retreated.

Needless to say, I didn't sleep at all the rest of the night. And in the morning, the spider monkeys began harassing me again. My least favorite rainforest creatures followed me back to the coca field. The racket they made would have alerted anyone checking on their crop.

No one was there, though, so I ventured out into the field to get away from the monkeys. They soon became bored and wandered off. The field was too big and the plants were too green and mature to try to pull it all by hand. I was not sure what to do, so I decided to follow the dirt road back to see where it originated.

The dirt road and old tracks left little doubt that most of the cars were turning south on Quintana Roo, which was the road that went through the tiny town of Nuevo Put. I left a few things on the road that would be disturbed if anyone drove over them, then headed south to get my car. Nuevo Put was only about six miles away, I guessed, but it took almost three hours to walk there. From the tiny village, I drove into the bigger small town of Xmabén for more bottled water and something for ant stings. For dinner, I went to a true dive of a place and enjoyed *the* best picadillo I have ever had.

The sun set as I drove back to the coca field. Using the headlights, I checked the things I had left on the road first, to make sure no one visited the field while I was gone, and then drove my car over every coca plant in that field at least three times. My tires slung mud everywhere and I laughed out loud as I did donuts like a teenager who'd snuck out in his parent's car in the middle of the night. Out in the rainforest, I heard spider monkeys throwing a fit, upset about being disturbed.

"Suck it, monkeys!" I yelled through the open window. "My turn!"

I burned a quarter of a tank of gas, but I completely destroyed their crop. Best of all? I didn't have to kill anyone.

Chaos

Everyone pretended to be into the loud, obnoxious Acid Jazz "music" that was abusing Al's ears. He wanted to arrest Qian as soon as possible and get the hell *out* of there, so he did not allow anything to distract him from his tasks. He watched his informant carefully. The Brit carried on several conversations with various people, but none were Asian. Finally, he sat next to a man at the bar and crossed his arms as he had indicated, one arm on top of the other.

Qian had immediately recognized Al from Turkmenistan and was way ahead of them. His hands were under the bar, so Al approached cautiously. Qian watched Al approach in the mirror behind the jagged line of bottles on the shelf and waited for just the right opportunity to exact his revenge. For the angry young man, this was more about enjoying the moment than actually eliminating his enemies.

As is the result in most quick-draw gunfights, the one who draws first is usually the winner. This shootout was no exception. Qian had his hand on his 9mm and had already switched off the safety.

Before Al could get his pistol out of the unfamiliar holster, he took two to the chest.

Chaos.

At such a close range, the projectile hit him with such brutality that it knocked him flat on his back, penetrating the substandard bulletproof vest. Al was sprawled out on the floor, unable to breathe, but still kept trying to draw his weapon as he watched Qian shoot the Brit twice in the chest and once in the forehead. People were screaming and scrambling away. The house lights came on and the bar became eerily quiet for a moment when the music stopped. Al managed to get the gun out of his holster, but Qian stomped on his wrist, pinning his arm to his bloody chest with a $700 pair of sneakers.

I'm going to die here in Lithuania, with no one left to identify my body.

With a childish smirk, Qian spoke loud enough for anyone hiding nearby to hear. "I'm going after your friends, next."

For a man with no heartbeat and a severed spinal cord, Al put up one hell of a fight. Still smirking, Qian deflected Al's weakened, left-handed blows with his other leg as if he were dancing, although he'd be bruised for days. The last thing the Turkish Special Investigator saw was a flash of fire emitting from the gun pointing at his forehead.

Wait, What?

"Shannon" lived with the guilt long enough. Her father's indiscretions could not be her problem any longer. And if she had to do time for multiple crimes, then so be it. If her father had to do *more* time for yet another crime, then that's the way it had to be. She was done. She hadn't spoken to her father in so long it might even be impossible to find him anyway. She made an appointment with an attorney to find out what would happen if she turned herself in.

When a legal assistant called out her name, it startled her and she nearly bolted. "Miss Williams? Mr. Davenport will see you now."

Mr. Davenport, an attorney for decades, had learned when to callously interrupt and redirect. "Miss Williams, please start from the beginning. When did you help your father defraud insurance companies and financial institutions?"

"Well, I was seventeen, soooo, that would have been 1987 or 1988."

"Okay, when was the *last* time you helped?"

"Oh, that was the first and last time. We gr– I grew up being part of his scams. It was the only life I knew. But the only time I actually *helped* him, I did so because he promised me a new car."

"Miss Williams, unless you committed murder or forgery yourself, the statute of limitations has long since expired."

"Wait, what?" She looked back and forth between the attorney and the legal assistant.

"If you are shooting straight with me, there are no arrest warrants for you. Frankly, there likely never was."

Shocked, Shannon sat in silence, unsure about what she was supposed to do now.

"What is your real name?"

Her brows compressed and she slumped in her chair. She had to admit something that was humiliating. "Um, I'm not exactly sure. I have no birth certificate. Or at least no real one. And every time I asked my father what my real name was, he would make up another name. Gertrude. Matilda. Gladys. That kind of nonsense. But, I kind of like the name I have now."

"Okay, that's fine. Do you know your real birthday? Or where you were born?"

"No." A wave of sad, hopeless regret surged through her body and settled in her reddened face.

"Well, don't you worry. My assistant here is going to help you get your birth certificate, driver's license and passport in order."

For-E-ver

Dr. William "Bill" Nogan-Wheeler logged in to his online brokerage account and saw that his balance had dropped from $8.3 million to $5 million. He also checked to see if his wife had full access to the account. Then he logged in to a new trust fund account and was pleased to see a balance of $3.3 million.

He set up the fund to reinvest twenty-five percent of the interest every month, which was designed to help compensate for inflation. The remaining seventy-five percent would be automatically deposited into a special scholarship account at the university where he earned the Master's Degree that got him into medical school. Every time the balance reached $20K, another scholarship would be awarded to some deserving student who needed financial aid. The amount of the scholarship would increase 8% per year to keep up with the rising cost of college tuition.

He was upset at how low the highest interest rate was for a trust fund, but that would go up over time as the Federal Reserve increased primary rates. At first, the interest earned would only amount to roughly $6,000 per month, however, Bill's new Anonymous Scholarship Fund would provide financial assistance forever. For-E-ver.

I still don't know who that man was, but I am grateful he happened along.

Moving On

I had completely lost track of time, but I did enjoy swapping a few emails with a curator at the Olmeca Archaeological Museum. She was interested in the Mayan ruins, but wasn't as excited about it as I was. She said that even though there were new discoveries at least monthly, they didn't have the budget to look into everything. She added that most of the Mayan artifacts that people found were not reported at all, but instead, get sold into private collections.

In my last email, I tried to buy her interest.

```
If I made a small donation to the museum, could
you send someone out to investigate my find?
It really looks special.
```

```
ES especial, pero todos los sitios mayas lo
son. Lo mejor que puedo hacer es ponerlo en la
lista, que es extensa. Entonces el sitio
tendrá que esperar su turno.
```

Translated, her bad news read, "It IS special, but all the Mayan sites are. The best I can do is put it on the list, which is extensive. Then the site will have to wait its turn."

That was unfortunate, but there was nothing more I could do, so I moved on.

Four more trips to the bank in Felipe Carrillo Puerto to buy cashier's checks, in as many weeks, had my investment balance up to almost a half million dollars, with about twelve percent of that being gains. My cryptocurrency investments were profitable, but everything else was mediocre gains or losses. I sold the losers and bought more cyber currency stocks. Still, no red flags.

Months had passed since I took out the last coca field, and while thinking about what day it was, I realized I had completely missed Thanksgiving, again, by two days. I stared out of my kitchen window, sipping my coffee and watching the new resort construction starting on the other side of "my" cove. Disappointing.

Absentmindedly, I noticed my reflection in the glass. Was that really me? Long hair. Bushy beard. I was obviously enjoying the life I had made since I had procured this property. And stopped killing criminals. However, the resort they were building on the other side of the cove changed things. Soon, the area would be crawling with tourists. Boats would be coming and going into the peaceful cove far more frequently.

With Carla's worn photo in my hand, the setting sun sealed the deal.

Time to move on. I'm going back to find her.

Decisions made, I took inventory of my resources, which were few in numbers, but high in quality. Besides a new phone, groceries, utilities, and gas, mostly for boat rides in the Chris-Craft, I hadn't spent much of the money I took from the cocaine manufacturers. I found I had a little over seven million in U.S. dollars and several stacks of Mexican bills with denominations of 100, 200 and 500 pesos, which was worth, maybe, fifty thousand or so in U.S. dollars. There were also several bags of coins that were too heavy to lug around for long. I didn't even bother to count those.

Early the next morning, I showered and shaved, and ate my last bowl of Froot Loops. I picked out the newest SUV on the property and loaded it with a duffle bag of my meager belongings, along with the stacks of paper pesos and the bags of Mexican coins. I packed the seven million U.S. dollars into two suitcases, but left the safe open so that anyone could see the Mayan artifacts and gaudy jewelry in it. I lovingly placed the keys to the Chris-Craft on the kitchen counter with a note that simply read, "Enjoy," in English and Spanish, but I took the keys to the house and drove away from my mini-paradise.

In Felipe Carrillo Puerto, I stopped for gas. From the pump I could see a large gathering in a park across the street that looked like a Sunday wedding reception. Strings of festive white bells swung above the heads of family and friends as they danced to live mariachi music. They were probably dirt-poor, but everyone seemed happy.

This is exactly why I brought the keys to the house with me. I wanted to return at least some of the resources the criminals had taken from the Mexican people.

I wonder if the father of the bride will accept a wedding present.

The bride's father wasn't doing a lot of smiling, but he didn't appear to be angry. He may have been stressed about seeing how his hard-earned life savings was being spent. Food, beverages, clothing. It adds up, but I could not know how he'd react if I offered him resources that he could either use or sell.

When his wife left the table to mingle, I walked up and sat next to the man, hoping the translation tool on my phone would help convey my intentions.

```
These are the keys to a house in Vigía Chico.
I have to abandon it all, as did the occupants
before me. Please accept the things there as
a gift to you and the newlyweds. If you do not
take or sell everything, it will all certainly
be stolen, or taken by a real estate agent.
```

There are also cars and even a nice boat, but collecting the resources quickly may be necessary.

At first, I didn't think he would accept my offer, but I pointed out that young couples need every opportunity to make it in today's world, so he took the keys, although he looked ashamed of himself.

The things decent fathers do for their children. Sometimes it takes true strength to push your way through the humility.

I wrote the address on a wedding napkin, patted him on the back, and left it at that.

Then I was off to Matamoros and Brownsville.

Brothels and Borders

There are a limited number of ways to sneak across the Mexican border into the United States. I could hire someone with a vehicle, plane, or boat that was designed to hide humans, but that might take weeks. Walking through miles of prickly pear mazes in extreme heat, while rattlesnakes coil underfoot might be an option. Or not. There are also hundreds, or perhaps thousands of tunnels under the border, but they are fraught with their own perils and well hidden, obviously. I didn't have a clue how to find one.

None of those options were viable or desirable. If I found someone who looked enough like me, I could use their identification to get across the border, and continue to use it for a while back in the states. I had some experience with that, and I had an idea where I might find a horrible person who looked enough like me for their driver's license and passport to get me across the border.

Sadly, finding a brothel in Matamoros that specialized in underaged prostitutes was far too easy. Girls, and I literally mean *girls*, were standing outside the establishment and on all four corners of the closest intersection. They all employed varying methods of enticement to try to rouse the interest of men passing by, and were successful far too often.

With growing impatience, I waited for someone who looked a little like me to approach the child hookers. My persistence paid off after sunset. Quite a few more men began hanging around the brothel, including a man who slightly resembled me, only shorter and a little sleazy-looking. He began negotiating a price with one of the younger prostitutes, money in hand. I got out of my car and stormed across the street through the light traffic.

"Hey! Come with me."

Startled, the guy took off running, so I tripped him by focusing on his legs. I bent over him and put my face within inches of his and hissed, "Do you want to live? Or do you want to die right here, right now?"

Too terrified to respond, he looked at me and simply shrugged.

"Come with me, get in my car. *Now!*"

He complied. The child prostitute never flinched. She just stood and watched. I turned the car around in the street and motioned for the hooker. When she approached the car I handed her the bags of Mexican coins. With a bag under each arm, she looked at me, confused. I suggested she go to America and spend that money wisely, like starting a small business.

Turning to the loser in my passenger seat, I asked, "Where's your car?"

The loser's beat-up compact car was parked about three blocks away.

"Keys." I extended my hand making my intent clear. He grumbled, but dug into his pocket and handed me his fob. The lights flashed when I clicked the lock button. I noted the crossroads, drove to the banks of the Rio Grande and parked in a secluded spot.

I looked the loser in the eye and scolded him. "That girl looked like she was thirteen. Would you want someone to treat *your* daughter like that?"

"Hey, those girls aren't so innocent. They choose to live this way, I'm just one customer of many."

"Then why did you run?"

"You scared me, man! Hey, don't knock it till you've tried it. Those girls are talented. They've all been thrashing mattresses for a while."

"They don't seem to mind?" I could barely contain my disgust.

"Not at all! They're hookers. Yes, they are young, but they're already professionals."

"So, you've been there before?"

"Of course! Nearly every weekend. It's legal here. If you're looking to hook up, try Luana first." With an irritating laugh he added, "They call her Doyawanna Luana."

"The kid looked thirteen."

He barked his last laugh, but did not get to finish his retort. "If they're old enough t– "

I took his wallet and passport, put rocks in his pockets, and dumped the dead child rapist into the Rio Grande. I drove back to Russell Reed's car and parked the SUV I was driving a few blocks away on a street with few lights. Even though it was probably a waste of time, I used wet napkins from a fast-food restaurant to wipe down the inside of Robinmahood's SUV. With the driver's side window down and the fob lying in plain sight on the console, I wasn't too concerned about an investigation.

Gone by morning.

Crossing the border during the day draws less scrutiny than crossing at night, so I drove to Playa Lauro Villar and slept on the beach. I would have gotten a good night's sleep if my mind hadn't been dwelling on all the men paying young teens for sex. Both Americans and Mexicans. Disturbing.

From Chris-Craft to Chris Cross

Long lines at the border crossing triggered some anxiety. Russell Reed's car was so poorly maintained the air conditioning didn't work. I rolled down the windows but the exhaust from all the other idling vehicles forced me to roll the windows back up. Waiting and sweating, I missed that SUV I had ditched. When I got close enough to the gates, I could see that the long lines were caused by border patrol agents checking each car thoroughly.

Great.

I used the time to memorize the information on Russell's driver's license and passport, and to attempt to make my hair resemble the 'do in his photo. Fortunately, the more I advanced, the faster the line moved. The guards were being less thorough than they had been, thankfully, but the wait was still stressful.

When I finally pulled up to the gate, I noticed the guard was looking weary and haggard, like maybe he had worked all night and all morning. Budget cuts? I felt for him, but his situation worked in my favor. He waved me through after a good long look at "my" identification.

The drive to Corpus Christi took about three hours because of heavy traffic, but the timing paid off. I happened to be in the right place at the right time to buy a beautiful sailboat from a guy upgrading to a luxury yacht.

He must have been on a power trip, or maybe he was just spoiled because the sailboat he sold me was quite nice, with a covered cockpit in the center, a modern kitchenette and roomy sleeping quarters in the hull of the bow. I gave the old man $120,000 in cash, which he didn't seem to mind. I figured he intended to save some money on taxes.

After I parked Russell Reed's car in a place where it would soon be towed and impounded, I wiped down the interior and outer door handles with alcohol wipes. I grabbed a quick bite at a nearby restaurant and then booked a ride-sourcing car back to my new sailboat. With the old song "Sailing" downloaded onto my phone, I put it on repeat and took her out.

Sunsets in the middle of the Gulf of Mexico are breathtaking. "They" say you can hear the sun sizzle when it appears to dip into the water. Despite turning off my music and the boat's chattering radio, I didn't hear anything. I blamed that on the continued ringing in my ears, so I just tried to relax and enjoy the spectacular view.

In the morning, I awoke to a gently rocking sailboat and nothing but the sound of waves splashing against the hull. I fished a little but didn't catch anything, so I thought better of making a beeline for the tip of Florida, which was over five hundred miles away. Instead, I stayed close enough to shore to pull in for groceries and gas. I sailed most of the way, although sometimes I wanted to relax and travel under power for a while.

Every two or three days I stopped for supplies. Galveston first, then Port Fourchon and Sarasota. When I rounded the Florida Keys, I sailed close to shore so I could get a good look at the beautiful beaches and quaint little towns.

Passing a yacht off the coast of Islamorada, I noticed a monster of a guy and an attractive woman in a tiny yellow bikini sunbathing on the aft deck. She looked at me, then she lifted her sunglasses with one hand and used her other hand to shield her eyes from the sun while she stared some more. She didn't wave like most boaters who get close enough to make eye contact, so I didn't either. There was nothing about the encounter that was out of the ordinary until after I had sailed by, then my mind made an association to memories from the past.

Huh, that woman looked a lot like Jeanna.

There was no way that could be true though. The coincidence was *so* unlikely. There is no way my New York business partner would be on an expensive yacht, in the same spot off the coast of Florida, at the exact moment I passed by, especially after being separated for so many months.

Nah. No way.

I shook off the notion and kept going.

Coincidence or Catastrophe?

"That dude sure is gettin' an eyeful."

Jeanna didn't care. If anything, guys ogling a forty-year-old woman was a welcome compliment, but she looked up anyway and could not believe what she saw. "That looks like my old boss." She continued to stare. "There's no way that's even possible, but it sure looks like him." She lifted her sunglasses with one hand and shielded the sun from her eyes with the other.

When the sailboat passed and the man could no longer see her, Jeanna looked into her boyfriend's eyes. "Let's go home. I need to make a phone call."

"Huh?" He looked at his phone. "I have a couple of bars on my phone, just use it." He simply did not understand the gravity of the situation.

"No, that guy is *totally* wanted by the FBI, and the phone number I need is at home. Please, we need to go right now."

Her behemoth of a boyfriend sat up with a sigh, but Jeanna snapped, "Wait!" She took a deep breath to help her calm down and added, "Wait until he is further away. I don't want to let him know I recognized him."

Jeanna fretted while she waited and stressed out all the way home. Special Agent Carla Bright did not answer her phone. The call went to voice mail.

"Agent Bright! Jeanna Doyen. I'm pretty sure I JUST saw my old boss on a big, blue and white sailboat off the Florida Keys, heading north."

Surf's Up

During my slow turn north up the Florida coast, I began making better time when a heavier wind kicked up. I also found the welcoming breeze refreshing. Within a span of five or six minutes though, a severe thunderstorm popped up out of nowhere off my starboard side.

Uh, oh.

I started the engine as the cool darkness of the storm enveloped me. Lightning flashed all around my boat while the accompanying blasts of thunder shook everything under my feet. The lightning was not only deadly-dangerous, the thunder hurt my ears with such intensity I had to abandon navigation long enough to retrieve cotton balls from the first aid kit to put in my ears.

Rain and wind swept into my covered cockpit and soaked me, chilling me to my bones. Temperatures had dropped from the nineties to what I guessed was a wind chill in the sixties.

Wish I hadn't turned off the boat's radio.

Between the blinding flashes of lightning, I studied the GPS unit on the dashboard to find a port to put into. Any port. I had a new appreciation for the saying, "Any port in a storm." I wiped the water off the screen and looked closer.

Hmm. I think I may be in The Bermuda Triangle. Great.

Before I could turn hard to port, to head into Miami's Biscayne Bay, a *shower* of lightning bolts smashed into everything around me. The pounding intensity of the thunder almost crushed me, further exacerbating the ringing in my ears, despite my makeshift earplugs.

Waves split and I tasted the saltwater that drenched me, even though I was already soaked with rainwater.

I have no idea how the lightning missed me, but it *had* blinded me! I couldn't see anything. Not even the light from the screen of the GPS.

The engine had died. I tried to restart it but the key did nothing.

While I waited for my sight to return, I sensed that the waves were increasing in size and frequency. I was tossed about, reminiscent of a rough roller coaster ride. I came out of my seat a few times, but I held onto the wheel and managed to stay put.

Worrying about what would happen if my boat sank or I was tossed overboard, my imagination ran wild. I had enough sense to swim with the wind and waves, but being sightless, what would happen when I got close to shore? Would I be slammed into a pier, or tumble over rocks? My anxiety leveled up.

Dim lights appeared, but I didn't breathe a sigh of relief. The lights were to my port side, coming from shore, and not on my boat at all. Relieved I wasn't blind, I realized that the onslaught of lightning must have knocked out my electrical system. Everything was completely dead.

Another bolt of lightning streaked above me and the painful clap of thunder worsened the ringing, yet again.

A powerful, unnaturally aggressive wave came over my starboard side and knocked me about half unconscious. The sea didn't care. Waves pitched my boat as if it were a child's toy.

Fortunately, the wind is blowing me towards land. At least I have one friend on this ocean.

Sometimes I could see the lights on shore, but most of the time I couldn't. The waves must have been enormous. I was almost glad I couldn't see them. The roar of the storm increased and my only friend on the entire ocean, the wind, turned against me, too. It hit hard as the gale assailed my boat. Her well-designed sails caught all the air they could, causing her to heel over onto her port side.

I scrambled out onto the wet deck, but my shoes lost traction with nearly every step. I held onto anything I could find with a death grip while I groped around in the darkness trying to find the main sail's winch. I managed to get two full turns down, but the wind surged even higher and laid her down almost ninety degrees.

The cotton balls in my ears absorbed rain and saltwater, causing them to ooze out and irritate my ears. The sensation was irritable enough to make me want to dig the rest out, but I couldn't. Both hands were busy holding on and turning the winch. The itching was so bothersome that it distracted me as another massive wave slammed into the exposed hull. The jolt tore one hand loose as cold, rushing water splashed its way over the boat and ripped me off my feet. The only thing that prevented me from washing overboard was a surge of adrenaline that gave me enough strength to grip the handle of the winch.

As I swung around in the pitch black, legs pumping wildly, I realized the rain was pelting me so hard it hurt. When my foot caught a rail, I stabilized myself enough to stop swinging out over the open ocean, but the stinging rain became worse.

That's not rain. That's hail.

Getting back in the cockpit and finding a life preserver became my highest priorities as I cussed myself for not putting one on at the first sign of harsh weather. And for not lowering the sails sooner.

And for turning off the boat's radio, which would have warned me about the approaching storm. And for buying a sailboat.

The size of the hail increased and beat me until I bled in several places. With the boat pretty much sideways and rocking violently, staying on my feet was a challenge. Normally, I would have used the stairs to get into the cockpit, but because "down" was now in a new direction, I had to step on the side of a shelf to get back in.

A sustained bolt of lightning diffused by clouds and heavy rain revealed hail punching dozens of holes in my sails.

That's going to be a problem.

With one foot on the sideways doorway and another on a shelf, I reached through the darkness, searching for anything that might support my weight, but another massive wave slapped the hull and shook me loose. My left shin smacked something hard on the way down and my head hit the wheel.

Cussing again, I checked my forehead. I didn't feel a gash, but I couldn't tell if the wetness I felt was water or blood. I recovered quickly and groped around through the pitch black in the unfamiliar cockpit enough to find the door to the storage.

Retrieving four life jackets. I put one on well enough to keep me afloat in case I fell overboard, and then did my best to tie others to my duffle bag and two suitcases of money.

The storm raged, but the boat righted itself, mostly. The same hail that beat me bloody probably saved my life by shredding the sails to pieces. I felt around and found a flashlight so I could search for the cheap first aid kit and doctor multiple cuts and scrapes. All I could do was try to wait out the storm and hope my sailboat was seaworthy enough to get safely to shore.

Freaking Bermuda Triangle.

Mother Nature answered with another increase in windspeed and hail size. I don't know how the cockpit windows sustained the heavy blows of baseball-sized chunks of ice. I expected the glass to shatter at any moment. The noise from the hail, the wind, and the thunder were overwhelming as they challenged each other to achieve new heights.

After a few stressful minutes, the hail turned back into rain and the crashing waves diminished to what I guessed were mere eight-foot waves. I breathed a sigh of relief, but then the fatigue set in.

My new but battered sailboat seemed a little sluggish in the swells, as if it were exhausted, too. I knew she took on some water, but maybe it was worse than I thought. If my electrical system hadn't been fried by lightning, the bilge pump would have had that water out quickly. It would have to be bailed out by hand, but having some bailing experience, I wasn't too worried.

I climbed back onto the deck and shined my flashlight through the rain. My jaw dropped from shock. She was riding so low the water was up to her riding strake. If the wind picked up again, she would surely capsize.

A dim light drew my attention to the stern. Whipping my flashlight around in that direction, I was shocked again. I was so close to shore I could see security lights well enough to watch the waves break on the beach.

Aw, Ds *and* Fs*, man.*

The wind had pushed my boat around so that the pointed bow was facing the oncoming wind, and her stern was heading straight towards the beach. This meant good news and bad news. I was close enough to swim to shore if the boat sank, but, sharks. The wounds from the hail were still bleeding, unable to clot because everything was wet.

I dashed back into the cockpit and dragged my two suitcases of money to the back deck and waited for the inevitable. I'd have to search for my duffle bag later, assuming I could survive this. I tapped my pants pocket to make sure my phone was there. If the rain hadn't already killed it, the upcoming swim to the beach surely would, but if someone were to recover the phone, they might be able to trace it back to several stashes of dead bodies.

The point in the surf where the waves were turning to whitecaps was just seconds away when a large swell raised the sailboat and moved me closer to shore by a few yards, still stern first. When the swell moved out from under me, the boat dropped and the keel dug into the sand below. I was jarred to my knees. Wood and fiberglass splintered as the keel penetrated the hull and pushed its way into the cockpit.

The hull was probably weakened by the lightning strike. If I had stayed in there, I'd be dead or dying right now.

Water surged up and over the transom and ripped the smaller of the two suitcases from my left hand. Millions of dollars tumbled out into the open water. I tightened my grip on the larger suitcase and took a deep breath as the ocean picked me up and swept me over the starboard side.

To conserve oxygen, I just let it happen. When I was away from the bubbling turmoil that used to be my boat, I swam like sharks were zeroing in on one of the many bleeding cuts on my shoulders, arms and scalp.

I thrashed the water with one arm and both legs, doing my best to hang onto millions of dollars in a suitcase. All that movement further opened my fresh wounds, which burned from the salt water. My increased heart rate pumped blood out of those wounds even faster. I was bleeding a free flow of shark attractant. The angry ocean was as black as the cloud-covered night, which made it impossible to see if sharks were circling.

Every few seconds an enormous wave would wash over me and swirl me around in summersaults. I sucked ocean water into my lungs and had to expend precious moments of being above water coughing instead of breathing. The struggle to breathe nearly caused me to lose my grip on the suitcase several times but I managed to hold on.

I had no idea if my ability to temporarily paralyze or kill mammals would work on fish, but I tried. I focused on the water around and below me, but found that it was distracting me from swimming. The more I focused, the slower I swam. The faster I swam, the more vulnerable I became. After an eternity, I felt my hand drag through sand.

As I tried to get to my feet, a wave slapped me down and I rolled. Sandy saltwater filled my eyes and mouth, and the suitcase was ripped from my hand. I splashed and groped around frantically, trying to find the bag of money but it was lost in the darkness. I scrambled to my feet again and tried to blink through the mess in my eyes. In the flash of more diffused lightning, I saw the bright orange of a life jacket bobbing in the waves. I splashed back out into the water and lugged the heavy suitcase to shore, despite the monstrous waves pummeling me.

The longest swim of my life had only lasted a couple of minutes. Exhausted and bleeding, I sat in the wet sand to catch my breath. The rain washed the salt and blood from my wounds. While I rested, I watched my sailboat rolling around in the surf, breaking up and scattering as debris onto the beach.

Maybe boats just aren't for me.

The storm moved on nearly as quickly as it had hit, and the moon squinted through a thin cloud cover. Something washing up and down with the waves and other debris caught my attention. I could not figure out what it was, although I had my suspicions. The object was not something I had seen in my new sailboat. I would have noticed something that was gray and six or seven feet long. The thing moved with the waves like a dead body, which troubled me. I stood and approached the thing cautiously. It was a shark. A dead shark.

I looked for my duffle bag and the smaller suitcase, but did not see either of them. That was unfortunate. That suitcase contained about two million dollars, not to mention the travesty of breaking up a nice set of matching luggage.

Miami Bound

Carla's coffee machine most often saw her in fuzzy socks, a long T-shirt and a phone in her hand. Waiting for the coffee to brew was a perfect time to check her email and messages, which helped determine what driving forces might rule her day. When she got to Jeanna's voice mail, her eyes grew wide and her heart rate increased.

She had her colleague and lead, Ken, on the phone in seconds.

"Agent Bright! What can I do for you?"

"Sorry for the early call and such short notice, but I need a few days off."

"Um, okay. How many days?" Ken was genuinely surprised. Carla had never asked for time off that wasn't planned well in advance.

"A week, probably, but maybe only three or four days."

"Can you be more specific?"

"No, not really."

Ken nodded. "You have a lead on your serial killer case, don't you?"

Carla sighed. "Yes. I know you need me to focus on the Rustin and Baylodge cases, but a reliable witness had eyes on this killer yesterday evening, so I need to move fast."

"Okay. Take all the time you need. No need to turn in PTO, just go. I'll take on those cases for now."

"Thank you. I'm heading to Islamorada, via Miami."

Snooty Does Not Mean Refined

The storm passed, but the dawn skies remained cloudy. Early morning beach joggers and walkers were beginning to stop and gawk at the wreckage of my sailboat. There was still no sign of the other suitcase or my duffle bag, so I moved my bloody self farther up the beach. One hotel had a first aid kit intentionally visible by the pool. No one was around so I reached over the gate to the pool, unlatched it, and helped myself to the kit.

While I was doctoring my wounds another light sprinkle began, giving me the chills. A few moments later a front desk worker came rushing out and popped open an umbrella. Not for me, though. The incensed overreactor covered his precious 'do from the rain and scolded me.

"*Sir!* This facility is for guests only. You'll have to leave immediately."

"Yes, I'm okay, thanks for asking. I just need a few bandages. The hail got me good."

"*SIR!* Did you not hear me? The supplies in this hotel are for *our guests*. Our *paying* guests. Leave the premises. Now."

I rolled my eyes. "Actually, I was hoping to check in after I got cleaned up. Do you have any higher end rooms available?"

"Sir, it is highly unlikely that *you* have a reservation." He whipped his phone out and shook it like he meant business. "I *will* call the police."

"Wow. Okay." Choose your battles. You can't kill someone just because they are mean. Most people would have offered to help. But in the unlikely event of the police responding quickly to a man using a first aid kit without permission, they would definitely ask for identification. "Can you at least recommend a hotel with a *friendly* staff?"

He didn't even try.

I was almost finished anyway.

"You know, being snooty does not mean you are refined," I said as I walked away. I felt *sure* my stinging words caused him personal trauma.

There was a souvenir shop a short distance up the beach where I found a backpack, a cap, and some clean clothes, including some funky pants with a bunch of zippered pockets. Perfect for stashing rolls of cash.

A convenience store sold pre-paid mobile phones and a coffee shop that looked like they didn't hate anyone served as a temporary office. A pre-packaged breakfast was mediocre, but I couldn't resist a cup of their dark roast named Bermuda. As the slow drizzle outside turned back into heavy rain, no other coffee had ever tasted so good.

What is the best way to get to New York? Buy another boat? No way. Bus or train? No thanks. A Harley? Rain. A car? Maybe. RV? You betcha.

Pointing North

This time, Jeanna wasn't wearing her usual retirement outfit; a bikini. Instead, she donned an old pair of sweats she hadn't worn since she lived in New York.

"Agent Bright! Come in out of the rain."

"Miss Doyen. Thank you. It's really coming down." The covered porch didn't help much with the wind from the passing storm still throwing fits.

"Thank you for such a quick response, but we could have talked on the phone. No need to come all this way."

"No, thank *you* for contacting me, and I'm here because *he* is here."

"Well, he wasn't here long. He was in a sailboat heading north, and if he didn't outrun this storm," Jeanna looked out a window at the pouring rain, "he could have been blown all the way back to Manhattan."

Carla quizzed her about the description of the boat and left in a hurry. On her way back to Miami, the traffic report on a local radio station also reported damage caused by the powerful storm, including a story about the scattered wreckage of a sailboat. This concerned her enough to call the Miami-Dade Police Department, who told her the boat was in many pieces, but could possibly match the description she gave. The officer also said that no bodies were found, but neither were any survivors.

Her heart sank, like the remnants of that sailboat.

Kids Are Expensive

There were far more RV trailers for sale in the area than motorhomes, but I didn't want to have to buy a truck, too. While the rain poured, I called all the motorhome ads in the RV Trader from the dry luxury of my coffee shop office. The third person I talked to had a small but luxurious off-brand Class A RV. We discussed details between startling claps of thunder.

"We didn't use it like I thought we would. We took trips to the Everglades and made rounds through several Civil War battlefields, but that's about it."

"It seems a little pricey. How many miles are on the odometer?"

"Only about fifty-five hundred, and we're only asking what we owe on it."

"Oh wow, okay. It really is—" A flash of lightning gave me a one-second warning before a crash of thunder rattled the windows. I heard it over the phone first, though, a split second earlier.

Hmm, he's close. "It really is still brand new."

"My wife kept the inside clean and I maintained the engine and the outside. The RV is immaculate. There is also a cleverly hidden gun safe and a street-legal scooter mounted on the back that I'll throw in."

I don't know how much engine maintenance you can do in less than six-thousand miles, but that safe would be perfect for stashing cash.

"Can I ask why you're selling it?"

"Well, to be honest," the old man chuckled, "I'm selling it because kids are expensive. Two of my three kids had to move back home.

One of them has credit card debt up to his eyeballs and the oldest moved her entire family into my basement so they could afford their two new car loans. I need out from under the RV payment, the insurance, and the monthly storage fee."

I considered the big picture for a moment. What did I care if I paid too much for an RV? I was spending someone else's money. "You're asking fifty-seven thousand dollars. Would you be willing to accept cash?" A clap of thunder punctuated my question.

The old man paused for a few seconds after the thunder was finished, probably weighing his pros and cons. "Well, I suppose I would."

We made arrangements for the transactions at an RV dealer off the Interstate, but the process took a couple of hours. The guy was so desperate for the money that he didn't even ask why I had it all in cash, or why the bills were a little wet. By the time we finished signing paperwork, my stomach was growling for some dinner. Also, it was a little late in the evening to try to get on the road, so I decided to wait until morning. There was no reason to try to get used to a new RV at night.

Inside Information

Carla stood in the wet sand under one of several pop-up canopies as a drenching rain added to her gloom. She looked through the debris that local law enforcement and clean-up volunteers had collected, and found a duffle bag attached to a life preserver. The contents were surprisingly dry so she considered herself fortunate that she found no identification or anything else that might be used to track him. However, she did pull a folded picture of herself from the pocket of a pair of pants.

An emotional overload nearly shook Carla to her knees. There was now no doubt that this boat had belonged to her long-lost lover. Did he die in the storm? Is he out there somewhere in the stormy waters of the Atlantic, clinging to a piece of wreckage with sharks circling?

On the bright *side, if he had enough time to put a life preserver on this duffle bag, he likely put one on himself, too.*

When no one was looking, she stuffed the photo into a pocket. She looked through the rest of the recovered items, but it was all just pieces of the sailboat.

After Carla stepped out from under the canopies into the rain, she walked down to the beach where wreckage was still being recovered. Two animal control workers were also attempting to load a dead shark into the bed of a service vehicle, but were struggling because of the size of the creature. She noticed no obvious wounds on the shark, which made her wonder if he had killed it using his unique talents, and if he killed the shark before or after it attacked him.

After the two men managed to get the shark into the bed of their truck, she showed them her badge and asked them, "Are you going to check that shark to see if there are human remains in the stomach?"

The older of the two, still huffing and puffing, and drenched from the relentless rain answered her between breaths. "We can, whew! If someone, requests it."

Handing him a card, she made the request. "When you know the results, can you call me immediately?"

He took off a glove and took the card. With her being FBI, he was eager to please. "Yes, ma'am."

Ugh. Please just stop with the ma'ams. She gritted her teeth and moved on without saying anything.

A beachfront hotel had a decent coffee shop with a clean bathroom. Carla locked herself in one of the stalls, took out the picture of herself she had found in the recovered items, and cried as she tore it into tiny pieces. She could not risk being connected to a serial killer. At least not yet.

As she flushed the bits down the toilet, she realized that she did not have a single photo of the man she loved. Now neither of them had a photo of each other.

That simply has *to change.*

Rocky Mount

I drove my new RV all day. Thirteen hours straight, with over two hours of that through a heavy downpour. Slow and steady on wet pavement or dry, always staying under the speed limit to reduce the chances of getting stopped by the police.

To help pass the time and stay awake, I called my author friend, putting the call through the sound system of the RV. We chatted for hours. I could hear him typing notes furiously as I caught him up on all that had taken place. He asked a lot of questions, many of them about the Mayan site I had found, but he also wanted to know every detail about the vintage Chris-Craft.

He was busy working on several other projects, but the first two of "our" books were selling so well that he wanted to put everything else on hold to write about my latest adventures.

I probably could have kept driving and talking, but when I saw Rocky Mount, North Carolina, I simply had to stop for the night.

Normally, I'd take the time to find the best spot to camp or park an RV, but it was well after midnight. A Walmart parking lot never looked so good. I parked, plopped onto the bed, and passed out.

Bright, early-morning sunlight penetrated my eyelids, waking me up long before I was ready. My mind was too foggy to get back on the Interstate, so I decided to have breakfast. I pulled the scooter off the back in case I needed to go through a drive-thru window, and took off in search of a place to eat.

Froggy

Carla's whole body jerked as her mobile phone woke her from a deep sleep. She was relieved to be awake though, as she was in the middle of that stupid, bad dream again. The final exams of a calculus class were about to start, but she had not studied at all. *Again*.

Shaking her head, she picked up her phone and fought the tangled charging cord for three full seconds. The call was originating from a local area code. She moaned and noticed her voice sounded like a bullfrog, so she cleared her throat.

"Agent Bright." Her voice still sounded like Satchmo.

"Um, Agent Bright?"

She cleared her throat again, more vigorously this time. "Yes, this is Agent Bright."

"Hi, Detective Ramon Morales. Sorry to call in the middle of the night like this, but you said to call immediately if something came up."

"Yes, of course, thank you. What do you have?"

"That sailboat was purchased by a Russell Reed almost two weeks ago in Corpus Christi."

"Russell Reed, Corpus Christi, got it." Carla committed it to memory.

"He also bought an RV just a few hours after the storm destroyed his sailboat."

Carla breathed a sigh of relief and wiped away instant tears from her eyes. She steeled herself before answering. "An RV. Okay."

He's alive! And an RV sounds semi-permanent, and *it sounds like he's headed for New York.*

"Yeah, he paid fifty-seven grand for the rig, all in cash."

"Okay. Do we have a description of Mr. Reed?"

"Just the photo on his Texas driver's license. The RV dealership had security video, but the resolution is too low for facial recognition."

"Thank you, detective. Could you email the photo to me along with anything else you have? And if you learn anything new, would you mind continuing to keep me in the loop?"

"Will do, and absolutely. Should we put out an APB for the RV?"

"No, not yet. Do you mind holding off on that? I think I know where he's heading and I'd like to get to him before he's spooked into hiding again."

"No problem. Let me know if you need that APB or anything else. It was a pleasure working with you." Detective Morales was eager to please.

With her mind no longer on the conversation, Carla answered with a knee-jerk reaction. "Thanks! You too!"

She quickly threw her things back in her bag while a single cup of hastily roasted Bitter-Brew® coffee dripped into a paper cup. All she could do was head north on I-95 and look for RVs matching the general description she had been given, which was a small, off-white, Class A with a paper dealer's license plate and a light blue scooter on the back.

Carla pushed the speed limit as much as she could without getting pulled over in her rental car. A highway patrol officer would likely let her off with a warning, but she didn't want the delay.

It would have been a waste of time to take every exit and check all the gas stations along the way, but she did drive through every rest area.

On the Interstate, she slowed down to look at the drivers of three RVs that closely resembled the description, but he was not driving any of them.

She drove all night, but when she saw Rocky Mount, North Carolina, she chuckled to herself and exited. Was it women's intuition? Or good detective work? Either or both, but only if she found him.

A quick search online revealed several places to park an RV overnight, and Carla cruised through each one with no luck.

The last RV park Carla checked was well outside of Rocky Mount, and the sun was already coming up. She gave it up as a lost cause and pulled into a coffee shop with a drive-thru window. She ordered a bucket of coffee, but when she pulled up to the window she smelled fresh pastries. Too wonderful to ignore, she added a blueberry maple scone to her order. As she waited for her treat to be heated up, she noticed a Walmart sign.

"No. No way. Maybe?"

SO Close!

Breakfast at a greasy diner was unsatisfying. I couldn't even finish my biscuits and gravy, which were borderline disgusting, so I stopped at a coffee shop on the way back to the RV.

"What'll you have?"

"Just a large, dark roast drip aaannnnd I'll try one of those blueberry maple scones."

"Oh, sorry. I *just* handed our last one to someone in the drive-thru."

"Aw, maaan."

Aiden turned and looked at someone cleaning the counter. "Allie, when you get a chance, could you erase the blueberry scone off the chalkboard?"

"You got it, Aiden!"

"Okay, I'll have the banana walnut muffin instead."

Atlantic City

One of several ocean yachts cruised by a beach just south of Atlantic City. None of the people on that beach paid any attention to passing ships, though. To do so would have meant looking directly into the bright, morning sunlight. When a young Asian man dove off the yacht, none of them noticed, and no one paid attention to him as he swam ashore and stood in the surf with a waterproof bag over his shoulder. With a major goal accomplished, the "undocumented immigrant" sat in the sand to catch the sun's warming rays.

When the man was dry, he walked the boardwalk until he found a fashionable clothing store where he paid for a few days' supply of clothes with one of several forged credit cards. An ATM was kind enough to give him three hundred dollars, which paid for a cheap mobile phone from the electronics store a couple of blocks away.

The next stop was a store with a luggage department, where he bought a large bag with big wheels. But then after paying for the worst excuse for Chinese food he'd ever tasted, he gave the credit card to a homeless old Asian man.

"Feed yourself well and buy some clothes, but then throw this card in the trash."

Sadly, the old man didn't buy food or clothes. He went straight to the liquor store and bought enough alcohol to drink himself to death that night, while Qian slept in a luxury hotel suite.

Dunking the Scone

Carla drove through the Walmart parking lot and gasped a little when she saw an RV matching the description she'd been given. Her heartbeat increased and her face flushed, hot and uncomfortable.

The cab was empty, so she knocked a timid rhythm on the RV access door. When no one answered, she knocked again with more gusto.

"Babe? It's me."

Hearing no response, Carla tried to look in the windows. At the back of the RV, she noticed the unlatched bike rack and realized he would probably be returning soon. She got back in her car and moved it far enough away to be inconspicuous, but still have a view of both the rear of the RV and the side door. She sipped her coffee and dunked her scone.

Gray clouds moved in, blocking the sunshine intermittently. As she waited, she caught herself nodding off a couple of times from sheer exhaustion, but shook it off.

And the Kitchen Table

As I was lifting my scooter onto the rack on the back of my RV, I noticed someone walking slowly in my direction. I could sense their eyes upon me. Were they just a Walmart customer returning to their car? Or were they approaching me? Without making it obvious that I knew someone was coming, I tried to pick up the pace on the tasks involved in securing the scooter in case I needed to make a hasty getaway.

I froze when I heard the most familiar of voices. "Babe? Is it really you?"

My face involuntarily snapped around in her direction. The last time I saw her she had been trying to arrest me. What was her intention now? Surely, she wouldn't call me "Babe" if she was about to cuff me. I stepped closer to her, scooped her into my arms, and slowly, slowly moved in for a kiss to see if she was receptive or hesitant. She was amenable enough to close the gap between our lips and kiss me like she had been missing me.

I hope I don't have muffin crumbs in my beard.

The prolonged kiss escalated into a passion that would surely lead to something more.

Wait a minute. She tastes like blueberries and maple. Hmmm. A question for another time.

Later that day we came up for air. But then we kissed some more. When we noticed it had started to sprinkle, we slipped inside my RV, where it did not take long to break in the new bed. And the couch. And the passenger seat of the cab. And the shower, which was challenging because it was so small.

For now, all was well.

Diamonds Are an Outlaw's Best Friend

While taking a breather, I showed Carla the safe full of cash and told her there was a suitcase full of money somewhere in the wreckage of a sailboat strewn on a Miami beach.

"I just came from there, but no suitcase had been found, or at least no one had turned one in."

"Oh, man. I tied a life vest to that bag, so someone is probably a couple of million bucks richer."

"A couple of *million*? Really? How much is here?" Carla nodded at the safe.

"About five million, I think. When I packed, I didn't count how much went into each bag."

With a cringe, Carla said, "Okay, Babe, we can't be carrying around all this cash."

I noticed she had insinuated that she had no intention of us being separated again. "Suggestions?"

Without hesitation, Carla proposed matter-of-factly, "Non-GIA diamonds."

"Okay. Uh, 'non-GIA' diamonds?"

"Yeah. No serial numbers."

My face scrunched up in disbelief. "Serial numbers?"

"All Gemological Institute of America diamonds have microscopic serial numbers lasered into them. Everyone knows that."

"Well, not *everyone*." *I'm just not a diamond guy. She is, though. Noted, for future reference.*

"Also, if you have anything on you that can be traced back to Russell Reed, you need to get rid of it right now. There's a warrant out for his arrest."

"Aw, hell. Even my alias has warrants. We need to ditch this RV then."

Carla looked around. "Okay, but we can't leave it here. Not with the rental I'm driving so easily traced to me."

I was accustomed enough with using aliases to always have contingency plans in mind. "No worries. I already have a solution in mind. Let's drop it off at an RV shop and ask them to change the oil and service the generator, but then don't go back for it. Just leave it there."

Her eyes brightened. "Good idea. At the very least, that'll put some time between us and anyone checking security videos."

Although I nodded an acknowledgment, I offered another explanation. "That's good, but what I had in mind was simply leaving it there with an amount due. When no one comes back to pick up the RV, the service center will file a title claim for an abandoned vehicle to recoup their investment. That way it never gets towed to the city impound lot. It never even gets reported as abandoned."

"Excellent! Easy."

"However, it's going to be a lot more difficult for me to get a new identity that's usable, especially for the long term. It's not an easy task. Takes time."

Slowly, Carla allowed a pleasant but undefinable expression to drift across her face. "I've given this some thought. I think I know of a legitimate way to get you a new, permanent identity."

"Yeah?" She had my full attention.

"The Witness Protection Program."

"What? Seriously?"

Nodding, she went on. "First, we arrange for you to 'witness' a crime of significant magnitude for you to be invaluable. Then, maybe, you contact a crime tips hotline and tell them what you saw and how you were involved, but will not agree to testify without immunity. Full and complete immunity, for anything you've ever done, *and* secure a spot in the witness protection program for life."

"Okay..." The overall plan sounded simple enough, but we both knew complications would appear in the details.

She continued. "There's an evil bastard at the top of a heroin and sex trafficking ring that some of my colleagues have been trying to identify for years. The heroin comes from Syria and the young girls come from unwanted children in Asia and runaway American teens."

I grunted in disgust. I *truly despise* animals that prey on vulnerable kids. "I'm all in to get this guy. *And* all his associates, but I do *not* want to go back to the Middle East unless we absolutely have to."

"I agree, but we think he is here in the U.S., so no need to go back there. This Syrian guy is slippery. He always manages to squeak away somehow before he can even be identified. No one in law enforcement has ever even seen him. Some believe a dirty cop is tipping him off."

A thoughtful head-tilt gave me a second to think. "Maybe I can force some information from enough of his underlings to get to him. Do you know of anyone who works for this Syrian?"

"No, I don't, but my co-worker and lead, Ken, has been involved with this case for so long that some of the people he put in jail have already served their time and are now out on parole. Twice, Ken has made me think that he might be receptive to bending a few laws if it meant getting some of the worst offenders behind bars. Now might be a good time to feel him out. See how he feels about getting on board with us."

"Maybe, but there's something relevant from the defense industry that may apply here. This point is stressed repeatedly, and stems from many extremely difficult lessons learned." I paused and leaned in for emphasis. "Risk increases *exponentially* with each person brought into the loop." I leaned back to signify its simplicity. "Can you just look at his files?"

"Oh, that's right, you once held a high security clearance. You'll have to tell me all about that someday."

I wish I could. "I will!" Changing the subject was the thing to do. "If we get this guy, are we bringing him in or framing him? Or am I just taking him out?"

Carla thought for a moment and crafted her answer carefully. "If I get the opportunity, I'm taking him in. And remember that there are three goals here." She counted them off on her fingers. "Taking this guy down. Preventing his organization from forging on without him. And getting you into witness protection with a new identity."

Gratuitous Yelling C.O.

"I DON'T CARE IF YOU DON'T HAVE THE BUDGET FOR IT. FIGURE OUT A WAY TO FIND KEMAL! USE NEXT YEAR'S BUDGET IF YOU HAVE TO."

Tourist Traps and Diamonds

I hadn't driven my RV long enough to become attached, so I didn't miss having a motorhome after we dropped it off at Harvey RV. I *did* miss having some kind of identification on me, even if the driver's license was fake. Not too long ago, over a period of months, I had been forced to travel from the Mideast, through Europe, across the pond, halfway through Canada, and into the United States without an ID or passport. It had made me a little squeamish about traveling through busy cities with no means of identifying myself.

We continued driving north in her rented sedan, but she had to do all of the driving in case we got pulled over. We took the scenic routes along the coast and talked along the way. We needed to catch up on the past eighteen months. When I mentioned I had found out the small business I once owned was no longer there, Carla acknowledged with a grimace.

"Uh, oh. What?"

"Yeah, about that. I wouldn't try to contact Jeanna if I were you."

"What? How do you know Je— oh. FBI agent and all. Right. But, why? We get along great."

"Not anymore. She is pissed. We had to interview her in the course of our investigation. I did it personally so that I could control the situation as much as possible."

"I appreciate that."

Carla winked uncharacteristically and resumed her explanation. "When I left her house, she only knew that we were pursuing you for questioning. Nothing more. But later, when they seized your half of the cash from the sale of your business and froze her bank accounts, someone explai—"

"Wait, I'm sorry, back up. Cash from the *sale* of my business? She sold it?"

"Yes. That's where all that money came from."

"All of *what* money?" I had no idea what she was talking about.

"What, you didn't know you had three million dollars in a trust fund waiting for you?"

"Uuuhh, no. I have three million in legit cash?"

"You *did*, yes." Carla somehow managed to pull off a sorrowful nod. "But the FBI confiscated it."

"Oh, man. And you froze her accounts, too?"

"Well, *I* didn't. They were going to seize her accounts and assets, but because she is a single mom and all, I convinced my boss to just freeze them until we figured out whether or not she was involved."

"I appreciate that, as well. Jeanna is as decent as they come, but I don't blame her for being mad."

"Having her assets frozen was bad enough, but she also thinks you are some kind of vicious serial killer."

"Oh." Knowing Jeanna thought that made me sad.

"So, I wouldn't try to contact her."

"Gotcha."

We stopped in all the touristy towns and visited the largest jewelry shops along the way, buying all the non-GIA diamonds we could find. She did not go anywhere with me where there might be security cameras, but she taught me what to say and what to look for in a diamond.

With Christmas approaching, all the small towns we visited were decked out in holiday lights and decorations. Classic songs played over sound systems in the town squares. Sinatra, Andy Williams, and the Vince Guaraldi Trio. The homey communities projected a warm and welcome sense of belonging that made me long for the cabin I had lost to the U.S. government.

One of those towns left a more lasting impression than the others—Ponte Vedra Beach. The city should have been thick with mosquitos, as half the town seemed to be swamp, but there were hardly any. Instead, it was a clean, quaint town with a couple of special interests. First, we ate at a semi-fancy restaurant called Medure.

All the local people we encountered were friendly. Carla struck up a conversation with the happy couple next to us, Dave and Beth. Good people, but when she introduced us as Clive and Julianna, I had a difficult time keeping a straight face. Under different circumstances, I felt sure that the four of us could have all become good friends.

The second special interest in Ponte Vedra Beach wasn't pointed out to me until after we had driven around and looked through some of the well-kept neighborhoods. When we got back on the road, Carla wore a wide grin and moved her head in a way that indicated she was talking about the town we just left. "We just drove past three homes owned by the U.S. government."

"What? Really?"

"Yeah. A 'safe' house ready to be occupied, and two more that already are. If you look on Google Maps, the homes are blurred out, which is a foolish, dead giveaway, but no one asked me."

Doing my best dry Spock, I said, "Fascinating." I don't think she got the reference. Either that, or she chose to ignore me, which is far more likely.

"The city council in that town is very open to cooperating with the federal government." After a little head tilt that might have been interpreted as a concession, she added, "And accepting a tax break in exchange for cooperating."

"So, you've been there before, setting up witnesses?"

She shook her head as she explained. "No, I've never been there before, or placed witnesses in safe houses anywhere, but the team I was on in DC did so occasionally."

We moved on, and over the next eight days, we successfully converted a little over four of the five-plus million dollars of cash, into non-GIA diamonds, *and* we had some interesting conversations.

Curiosity got the better of me one day, so I asked Carla about an old wound on her back. "That scar looks like it was painful. What happened there?"

"This scar is how I got my promotion from just plain-Jane Agent to Special Agent."

"Do tell."

"The short version is, the FBI chased a guy named Nickolaou for years but couldn't catch him, so the case went cold. I caught it because, as you know, I excel at solving cold cases. I worked the case for weeks, but I totally found the guy. I tracked him to a dock in Boston and confronted him, but he tackled me like a linebacker. A jagged piece of concrete gouged me. I was a bloody mess, but still took him down."

"Wow. You are tough, Carla. *Truly* a badass."

I felt the need to share a story of my own, and began telling her about floating down the Vltava River in the middle of the night. When I got to the part where I encountered the white-water rapids, in the pitch black of night, the incredulous look on her face made me stop.

"Why the face?"

"I read The Attuned, Babe. I know all about that boat ride."

"Oh, right." I wasn't sure if I was disappointed or amused.

"You haven't had the best of luck with boats, have you?"

"You wouldn't say that if you had gone for a cruise in my old Chris-Craft."

Carla conceded with her *okay, whatever* face and a smile. She probably correctly assumed she'd read about it in the next book.

During those eight days of exploring east coast towns and tourist traps, we often sat on the decks of restaurants overlooking bays or the Atlantic Ocean. The waves and wind made it easy to brainstorm without being overheard while we discussed ways to get me close to the mysterious Syrian.

After one such discussion, and over dessert, Carla cheerfully said, "This is the best Christmas Eve I've had in a long, long time."

"Me too!" *Aw, hell, is it Christmas Eve?* "What would you like for Christmas, my love?"

"I got my Christmas present early."

Oh, that smile. That delicious smile. But she knows. She knows I had no idea today was Christmas Eve and she is just letting me off the hook. I don't deserve her. I have to sneak off later and get her something.

Focused on Revenge

Qian could think of nothing but exacting revenge upon the enemy known only as Sciens, even though he hated calling him that. "Sciens" was supposed to be *his* title, and no one else's.

He intended to kill the man and torture everyone his enemy cared about. He suspected that the FBI agent and the INTERPOL representative who came to investigate the slaughter of his colleagues knew Sciens personally. He just knew these things. The look in the dying INTERPOL agent's eyes and his violent reaction to the threat he'd made against the Turk's friends reinforced his opinion, and his need for revenge. Killing the investigator had satisfied his bloodlust for days, but that had been almost two weeks ago.

Two sets of automatic doors swung open as he stepped into the FBI offices in Atlantic City. A whistling, older man was leaving as Qian walked through the tiny lobby between the doors. He didn't recognize the tune to the theme song for Get Smart, so he didn't catch the reference. The whistling just irritated him.

A security guard behind a desk waved him over, where he introduced himself as Shirong Chen.

"I need to speak to FBI Agent Bright about a suspect she is pursuing."

"What's this about?"

With increased irritation, Qian spoke slowly, as though the security guard was a child. "As I said, a suspect she is pursuing."

"What suspect?"

"Excuse me?"

"What's the name of the suspect?"

Qian bristled. "I don't know the name of the suspect." More forcefully, he spat words between short pauses. "Agent, Bright, please."

The security guard clicked his mouse over and over, but eventually gave up.

"There is no Agent Bright in this building."

Qian figured as much, but hearing it didn't ease his irritation. "In, which, building, might I, find her?"

More mouse clicking finally led to an answer. "Long drive from here. There is only one Bright, and that's *Special* Agent Carla Bright, who works in the Jacob K. Javits Federal Building in New York City at 26 Federal Plaza."

"Now, was that so hard?"

A cold glare was the only response Qian received.

Bright and Surly

Carla hated to disturb Ken. He was focused on something. As his eyes were scanning back and forth on a file, the definition of the lines in his forehead and crow's feet became more and more pronounced. She paused a few steps from his desk to let him finish reading.

Aware of someone watching him, Ken looked up, surly at first, but his expression changed when he saw Agent Bright.

"Hey, Carla. How was your vay-cay?"

"Sorry to interrupt, Ken. You look busy."

"I am *very* busy, but I always have time for you."

She smiled her appreciation. "My vacation was perfection. All expectations were exceeded."

"Yeah? Your favorite place?"

My co-workers know too much about me. "No, this time I went in the opposite direction, where stormy weather gave me time to think about some of our cases."

Ken was curious. "Okay, you're going somewhere with that, right?"

"I am. I think we may have some overlap in a couple of cases we are working."

"Yeah?"

"Yeah. Do you think you could spare me some time tomorrow to talk about your Syrian sex trade and heroin case?"

"Absolutely, Carla. I can spare some time to talk about that right now."

"Ah, thank you, but I need time to review your file first."

With an odd expression of disbelief, he stepped over to his file cabinet, pulled a huge file out of a drawer, and dropped it with a solid thud onto his desk. "You're going to need more than a day to review this case. There is a lot more online, too."

Realizing it would take more time than she had anticipated, she asked, "Wednesday, then? The conference room with the large monitor?"

"I'll have a fresh pot of coffee ready."

Carla Bright asked, "Bright and early, then?"

Ken nodded and succumbed to his need to finish plowing through the documents on his desk.

Legal Now

A proudly-tearful Shannon stared at her first legitimate Social Security card. Having a valid one didn't quite seem real. She placed the card in a lockbox with her first genuine birth certificate, secured the lock, and slid her treasured possessions under her bed.

Now I need to find Chip and try to mend my calamity.

Philly Stakeout

Reading every page in the bulging folder that Carla got from Ken took days. And there were nearly as many reports online, all of which were dry and boring. She hand-wrote notes in a separate notepad and organized her thoughts according to whom we could target.

She met with Ken that Wednesday morning, as they had planned, and made more notes from his input.

Carla could keep track of everything in her head, mostly, and would rarely look at her notes again. The act of writing down her thoughts was usually enough for her to commit the information to memory. I couldn't do that, so I downloaded an open source, SQL database to my phone, imported the text from all the online data and, using speech-to-text, added notes from the hard-copy files. With all the text in a single, simple table, one sentence or line per record, I was able to search the data and cross reference quickly.

Between my data mining and Carla's instant recall, we determined the best place to start. We were going to target a despicable man in Philadelphia who loved underage girls. He'd been seen with different teens many times, but they didn't stay with him long. We guessed the girls did not stay long because it doesn't take long to get addicted to heroin.

We took New Year's Day off to relax and decompress, but late the next evening I found him at a known, favorite hangout of his. I followed and watched that miscreant for three days. On the evenings of the second and third days, I saw him with his arm around a girl who could have been twenty years old, or fifteen. There was no way to tell. I wanted to drop him immediately, but I knew to wait and let him lead us to wherever he was taking her. There could be more girls at his destination who needed help.

On that third evening, a man wearing dark sunglasses and driving a black Mercedes picked the two up and sped away. I texted the license plate to Carla with a brief description of the situation. Over an hour later, "Miscreant" returned, alone.

Carla called me that night. "Can you get some photos of your guy and his license plate? Also, see if you can get an address where Ken can pick him up at some point?"

"I already have most of that, including a home address and what I'm assuming is a work address, but I don't know if he even owns a car."

"Okay, thanks. Ken has the guy in the Mercedes under surveillance, and he made that happen with no questions asked."

"Excellent." I was relieved that Ken seemed to be on board with our efforts, but in reality, he was probably grateful for getting help on this case.

"Also, come home. Come back to New York." Carla genuinely sounded like she missed me.

"I'll be home in time for an early breakfast."

Before I headed back to New York, I seriously considered swinging by the miscreant's place to kill him in a most unpleasant way. But I didn't, despite believing I'd regret leaving him alive. Or at least someone would.

Still Catching Up

After a little monkey business, Carla was *all* business.

"They found the Mercedes by staking out the address where the car was registered, but the driver was alone."

"Aw, geez, Carla, give me a couple minutes here, will you?

She just laughed and went on. "Apparently, he's just a delivery boy."

Okay, we must be switching gears here.

"Did they look at the GPS history in the car or use his mobile phone history to see if they could figure out where he took the girl?"

"Not without a warrant, no."

"Ugh." I thought for a moment. "What if someone stole this *delivery boy's* car? And his phone? Could you track his location history then? If you found a phone in a stolen car, you could access these records too, right?"

"Well, yes, but that is too risky. Just stay away from him."

"You betcha. But just in case someone really does steal his car, can you have your fellow agents ready to retrace his route? Can you just have some peeps ready?"

She gave me a look.

"Carla, the rest of that girl's life could be at stake, and possibly the lives of others, as well."

She sighed and shook her head. "Yes, I know. And I realize there is nothing I can do to talk you out of this, so *please* be careful, okay?"

"I will be very careful, but please make this task easier for me by texting me the address of the Delivery Boy?"

Even though she hadn't fully stopped shaking her head, she sighed again and muttered, "In for a penny, in for a pound."

Streetlamp Shadows

A bus dropped me off several blocks from Delivery Boy's apartment in the Stenton neighborhood of Philadelphia. A brisk walk late on a cool evening was refreshing and led me to reminisce about hiking through the Canadian wilderness. I wondered which was more dangerous at night. The streets of Philadelphia? Or the bear-filled Canadian woods? Hard to know.

The Mercedes looked out of place in the parking lot of an old, featureless apartment complex. He was probably the type to try and impress people with fancy cars and suits, but never had any guests over for dinner.

A corner streetlight lit the parking lot fairly well, but across the narrow street were tall, established trees that lined a shadowy sidewalk. There were plenty of places to hide.

I wonder if I can set off his car alarm just by kicking a bumper.

One medium test kick on the back bumper set off the alarm. The horn was louder than I had imagined, which startled me.

Laughing at my own foolishness, I dashed across the road and hid from the light of the streetlamp. From behind a tree, I watched the blinds split in several windows as people checked on the racket, but only one of them opened twice, and then the alarm stopped.

Hmm, okay. That was a lot easier than I thought it was going to be.

Delivery Boy's apartment was easy to find. He was next to the main stairwell on the second floor. I knocked lightly on the door.

"What the hell do you want?"

"I've a word from New York."

He paused, but then insisted I leave, using more curse words than not. "And stay away from my car!"

"Is this really a conversation you want to have through the door, with neighbors listening?"

A brief pause was punctuated by the sound of a deadbolt unlocking. The door swung open and the boxer-clad Delivery Boy stepped back with a gun pointing at my gut.

As I stepped in, I whispered, "Do not point that at me."

He didn't comply, so I focused on his mind. Harshly. He collapsed into a rag-doll heap on the rug, and I shut the door before any neighbors had the chance to investigate.

I wanted this pedophile dead anyway. But I didn't want his death to be tied back to me, so I went to the kitchen and found an oven mitt to use to turn on the cold water in the bathtub. I drug him in as quietly as possible, and when the water was deep enough to cover his head, I did gentle compressions on his abdomen and chest to fill his lungs with water.

The tub full of cold water would cool his body down quickly and possibly cause a misleading, or at least ambiguous time of death, as investigators would assume the man got into a *warm* tub of water. The water in his lungs would likely misdirect the coroner on the cause of death, or at least cause some speculating. But there would not likely be anything in the report that might catch the attention of the FBI.

His phone and key fob were easy to find, but I searched his sparse apartment thoroughly for guns and drugs so that I could leave his front door open. In addition to the gun he had held on me, there was another in a cheap nightstand.

There were also fourteen one-hundred-dollar bills in his wallet, plus seventy-eight more in small bills. I took all but twenty-eight dollars and placed his wallet back on his dresser. There were some large plastic take-out bags in the kitchen, so I double-bagged his guns and phone, hoping to give the appearance of carrying leftovers. When no one was in the hall or pulling up in the parking lot, I slipped out of his apartment, leaving the door wide open.

Back in New York, I parked the stolen Mercedes in a parking lot in West Village with his phone and guns in the glove compartment. Carla became upset when I called. She was already grumpy about being awakened at 2:10 am, but when I told her he was dead in the bathtub...

"You *killed* him?"

"Well, it's not like I planned it."

"I'm not so sure about that." Carla had fewer filters when she was troubled.

"Okay, it's not like I planned to kill him *last night*. I was justifiably concerned that he'd shoot me in the gut. Can you just get people on this right freaking now, so we can determine where he dropped off that girl?"

"Yes."

The call dropped. She was pissed. I could tell. I counted on her to get over it though. Our endeavors occasionally required drastic measures. That's just the way it was.

Another Interrupted Lunch

My phone rang as I looked over a lunch menu. The caller ID reported "Private," but I took the call anyway. I just listened at first, waiting for whoever was on the other end to say something.

"Hello?" Carla asked in a hushed voice.

"Carla? Are you okay?"

"Yes, but I have to make this fast. We think we found the place where the girl, or girls, are being held. Right now, we are establishing a two-block radius of surveillance. Two local cops are going to knock on the door, and hopefully, the two men who are there will flee out the back–"

"What the..."

She was talking so fast I wasn't sure that I understood her. "Yeah. They want to follow them. We need you, the anonymous tipster, to identify the girl you saw with your Delivery Boy. Can you do that for us?"

"Yes, but it'll have to be over a video call."

"Of course."

"And I'll need a one-use phone so there's no history or tracing."

Still whispering, Carla slowed down. "Absolutely. But Babe?"

"Yeah?"

"The clock is ticking. Can you get your phone and still be in Long Island City in forty-five minutes or less?"

"I can try."

"Text my burner when you get your phone and I'll send you the address. Hang back, wait for us to enter the apartment, then call me after four or five minutes."

"Got it."

I took the subway, but I didn't have time to get a new phone, so I texted Carla and got the address on the way to Long Island. As I stepped up to ground level, I put my phone to my ear and used that faraway, caller's gaze to scan the crowd across the busy street. Ken was *so* FBI he was easy to spot. Black suit, white shirt, blue tie with white stripes, and a clean-cut haircut.

Carla made eye contact with me, turned her back to Ken and mouthed *"Five minutes."*

A Brooklyn police cruiser pulled up and double-parked next door to the building where Ken and Carla stood. Two officers got out and rushed in. Ken spoke into his radio several times, then they ran inside, too. I set a timer on my phone for five minutes and stepped around the corner to wait.

Locked Eyes

Young Qian was still learning to be patient, but hatred makes patience even more difficult to manage. The superhuman effort it took him to simply wait and follow *Special* Agent Bright had paid off. There in the alley with him, barely twenty meters away, stood the murderer who killed *every* one of his colleagues and many of the students he had recruited. *And* effectively destroyed his beloved university.

Qian flashed back to that day, as he often did, and wished he could go back in time and change his reaction. He had gotten upset and stomped out of the meeting just moments before Sciens murdered everyone in the room. Had he stayed, he could have lived out one of the many fantasies he had created since then. The cocky young man *knew* he could resist the powers of Sciens and overtake him, saving the lives of his colleagues and all those innocent students.

Remembering their deaths brought him back to the present. Angrier and more impatient than before.

He started the engine of the only weapon he had at the moment and eased out from behind the dumpster. As he slowly approached the object of his hatred, Qian locked eyes with Sciens and acted on his anger and impulses. When he was a mere five or six meters away, he stomped on the accelerator. The powerful SUV lurched forward, tires squalling dramatically.

Bricks and Sugar

I watched the other end of the alley as I waited to make my call. No one who looked like they were running from the cops went by, but a big, pearl-colored SUV pulled out from behind a dumpster and headed straight for me.

The vehicle wasn't just rolling down the alley, the driver was coming directly towards me. I looked at the man, who may have been looking at me, and a hint of recognition registered somewhere in my mind. As I tried to place the face, the SUV roared at me with obvious ill intent.

While scrambling back around the corner, I nearly knocked down a lady walking a tiny fur-ball of a dog. At that same moment, the SUV crashed into the corner of the building. Sharp pieces of brick flew onto the sidewalk and bounced off parked cars. The driver never took his foot off the gas as he powered into the busy street.

The SUV bashed its way into traffic, side-swiping a smaller SUV going in the other direction. Two cars skidded to a stop but a third tailgater rear-ended the second car.

Cops and FBI agents were already on their radios as I tried to calm down the lady I had run into. She and her dog both thought I was trying to attack them. She screamed, focusing her tantrum onto me, despite witnessing the SUV nearly run over all three of us. The little pup had me by a pant leg, shaking its tiny head back and forth while I tried to calm them both down.

The SUV turned the corner and disappeared, with no chance of me following it. Two police cars lit their lights, taking off after him with their sirens blaring, echoing between the tall buildings and abusing my ears.

Finally, the lady calmed down and tried to convince the tiny but vicious dog to let go of my pants. Bystanders gathered in nanoseconds and looked on like *I* was the bad guy... the one being attacked by a puny dog. A particularly self-righteous onlooker felt the need to show his superiority by scolding me. "Do *not* hurt that little dog!"

I gave him my best sarcastic shrug, and then signaled for him to leave with a gesture from my thumb. He walked away muttering something disparaging under his breath. Again, I couldn't help myself. I focused on his right thigh as he stepped off the curb and blamed it on karma. He took quite a spill.

"Sugar! Let go!" The lady gently tugged the leash, but the dog continued growling and shaking my pant leg. She reached down and hooked a finger under his collar. One good yank got "Sugar" off me, but the little bitch turned around and snapped at the owner, too.

"Sugar! No!" The relentless creature curled her lips to expose tiny, sharp teeth while growling an impressive warning. The lady recoiled in fear.

I had to laugh. Evidently, the woman's pet was the dominant partner in that relationship.

Whatever. I needed to focus on what had happened.

Who the hell *just tried to run over me? He looked familiar. And* why *was he trying to kill me?*

Okay, I could think of a lot of reasons why someone would want to kill me, so I needed to try to remember where I had seen him before. The problem was, I'd seen a *lot* of people over the past few years that had reason to hate me.

Also, no one but Carla knew I was here. No one would know to wait for me in that alley. *I* didn't even know I would be there. I guessed that he had to be involved in the human trafficking organization we were targeting.

Then the timer went off on my phone. The call! I needed to call Carla. It didn't take long to video chat and identify the girl I'd seen, so when we hung up, I texted her as I walked back to the subway.

`Someone just tried to run over me in the alley.`

`What? are you ok?`

`Some Asian dude in a pearl white SUV.`

`ok hang on, let me get away from everyone so I can call`

`K`

My phone rang before I got to the subway stairs. Without waiting for me to finish saying "Hello," Carla spat words fast, but in a hushed tone.

"Start from the beginning. What alley, why were you there, and when did this happen?"

"When you and Ken went in, I moved to the alley next to the building to get away from all the people in the street."

"And?"

"And he was already there, parked, and apparently waiting on me. He started his SUV as soon as I was in the alley. Then he pulled out from behind a dumpster, slowly at first, heading straight for me. He wasn't simply rolling down the alley, or exiting the alley, he was coming straight towards *me*, and he was looking me in the eye.

When he got about fifteen or twenty feet away, he gunned it and I scrambled out of the alley just in time. He crashed into the building where I had been standing, but bounced off and kept going, and then Sugar got me."

"Sugar? What? What do you mean? Never mind. Did you get a good look at the driver? Can you identify him?"

"Maybe. He looked familiar. I remember him from somewhere, I just can't place him. I'll tell you about Sugar, later."

"Okay, just... what did he look like?"

"Well, like I said, he was Asian, mid-to-late twenties. I have no idea how tall—"

"Wait! A young Asian man came looking for me at the Atlantic City office a couple of weeks ago. He told the security guard he had information on a case. He was told which building I worked in, but he never came by.

A question popped out of my mouth before I realized how obvious it was. "Can you get the security footage? Does it still exist?"

Carla answered with another question. "Do we need to?"

I wondered what she meant but said nothing, in case her meaning came to me later. It did not.

Playing Spoons

Chip was back in the casino at the All Inn, at his favorite Texas Hold 'Em table, earning next month's pay from unsuspecting tourists. He was not particularly fond of taking money from people vacationing in his beloved Bristlecone Springs, so he was careful not to wipe out anybody completely. He felt like he had already taken plenty from the three at his table, so when he got the sudden urge to visit the teahouse and ice cream parlor where he'd first met Shannon, he made up an excuse about playing through dinnertime and being hungry. He gathered his scattered chips and cashed them in.

Inexplicably drawn to the table on the back deck where he had first met Shannon, he sat and sipped his herbal chai tea. He had not been back to this teahouse since before they left for Vienna, where she disappeared. He had felt sure that coming here would pile on more depression, but even sitting in the same seat where he sat that day did not stir up any ill feelings.

He sipped his tea slowly and waited because his intuition told him something grand was about to happen. What could this tiny mountain shop offer him that would draw him away from easy targets at the poker tables?

What am I doing here? What good could possibly come from reliving memories of Shannon?

He shrugged and watched the late evening shadows dance in the pine and aspen treetops, highlighted by a brilliant orange backdrop. He was wondering if something was about to change his life when he heard the silky-smooth, sexy tone of Shannon's voice.

"Chip?"

Without turning around, he closed his eyes and fought back joyous tears. A whisper was all he dared let escape his lips. "Shannon."

"Please forgive me, and... well, let me try to explain?"

Chip turned to see if she was really there, and despite being overwhelmed by her rare beauty, he was calm and knew everything was going to be okay.

Shannon joined him at "their" table and summarized the unique situation about her father and brother both being con artists, and not speaking to either of them in years. She explained how she had been forced to change identities so many times growing up that she could not remember her real name.

Living a life of fear because of her family's actions had caused her to be secretive and suspicious, but her love for Chip had prompted her to hire a lawyer and turn herself in. It was time to face the music. However, the lawyer told her she had no legal issues, and certainly no reason to be on the run. Chip listened, sipped his tea, and became dumbfounded by the life she had led.

"I was afraid I'd go to jail, and maybe take you down with me. Can you ever forgive me, and will we ever be okay?"

"Already forgiven, Shannon. I understand. And I promise, everything is already okay. I love you, and I need you. My life is miserable without you. Mis-er-*ah*-ble."

They went home and made love. Then Shannon snuggled in for some skin-to-skin spooning, making herself indispensable. Again.

Chip slept better than he had in months. Shannon slept better than she had since she was a child.

Just Handle It

"So, umm, about Long Island." Carla's inflection suggested a good-news-bad-news scenario.

Something bad was coming, I was sure of it. "Yeees?"

"Two things."

"Yeeeees?"

"Our efforts in Long Island last Monday saved *three* girls, temporarily, at least, *but* our efforts to infiltrate the underage sex traffic ring did not happen like we had hoped. They followed those two suspects, but they both just went straight home, *get this*, to their *families*. We arrested them this morning and questioned them extensively, but they revealed nothing. Neither of them even admitted to being there."

All I could do was shake my head in disbelief.

Carla went on. "Long Island was a bust. A waste of resources. However, I watched the video of the Asian man that came looking for me in Atlantic City."

"Yeah?"

"It was Qian."

"Who? Chee-un? Who is that?" She acted like I should know that name, but I had no idea who she was talking about.

"It's more like 'key' than 'chee.' Key-un. Do you remember a young Asian man at the 'university' in Turkmenistan?"

Carla's reminder triggered a memory for me. "There was a cocky Asian man there at first. He got ticked off about something and stomped out like a child."

Nodding, Carla said, "Sounds about right. Well, apparently, he's still ticked."

"I *knew* I'd seen him before. I can't believe he survived that day. Well, that's just great. And somehow, he found me?"

"He found *me* because he knew I was in the FBI, and then followed me to find you."

"Oh, man, if I ever see Al again, I'm going to beat him unmercifully at a game of chess."

"We are going to have to watch our backs, twenty-four-seven. There's a good chance he followed me home, too, so we need to assume he knows where I live."

I tossed out an idea. "Is there any chance you can move into one of those safe houses? Are there any around here?"

"Not without full disclosure to my colleagues. I thought the same thing, briefly."

After being lost in thought for a few minutes, something occurred to me. "Maybe we can use this to our advantage. If we know he is following you, or might again in the future, maybe we can set him up."

"Maybe. We might also need to involve Ken."

That idea didn't appeal to me at all, but I put it on the back burner. "Can we keep Ken in mind, but not get him involved yet?"

Her face soured, but she accepted it. "Okay."

Refocusing our attention on the data we had on the criminals, one loser bubbled to the top of the muck. He had been accused of child molestation twice, but no one could prove anything. However, both of the men Carla's team arrested that morning were known associates of his, which sealed his fate.

Carla was so disgusted with how the situation with the two men in Long Island was handled, she vented. "I *hate* that those two Long Island suspects were allowed to slip out the back. Everyone now understands that, as soon as they were away, they called their contact and warned them that they were caught."

"Yeah, that was either a colossal, rookie-like mistake, or the person who made that stupid decision is somehow involved."

She was noticeably shocked. That thought had obviously not occurred to her. She had always assumed that if a leak existed, it would have been a "lowly" cop or administrator, not someone higher up. After a moment, she reluctantly made a suggestion. "Maybe we leave law enforcement out of this one."

"I am *so* okay with that."

"Just, handle it. Either infiltrate the organization or wring the information right out of their– "

"Okay! I got it." The way she continued wringing some unseen object with her hands made me uncomfortable enough to squirm.

Bottom Rung

He was clean shaven and his shoes were shined. He wore a pressed button-down with a power tie and a nice sports jacket. You just never know. I followed him from the law office where he worked in Westbury to an office building in Huntington. I lost him for a few minutes when he entered the building, but after I found a place to park, he wasn't hard to locate. The pedophile was standing in the lobby talking on his phone, or pretending to, while he looked through the windows of an onsite daycare facility.

Knowing his history, I wanted to drop him dead right there, but I didn't. There was a remote chance he actually had a child in daycare. Seeing him watch those children made me sick. I kept thinking about taking him out immediately, but I waited, just to be sure. When he left a few minutes before the daycare closed without picking up any kids, I felt better because I knew he'd never abuse another child.

I made a promise to myself. *He will never hurt another child.*

As he got into his car, I jumped in on the passenger side and paralyzed him from the neck down. It was a struggle to drag him into the passenger seat, but thankfully, it was already dark outside. No one on the busy street seemed to notice. Either people could not see through the tinted windows, or they did not wish to be involved. I kept him paralyzed as much as possible, but I had to let him breathe a little. Still, I managed to get him buckled tightly into the passenger seat, and then used one of his shoelaces to tie his hands together.

"You won't be needing this anymore," I informed him as I bent-paperclipped his SIM slot and removed the card. I then drove to an area of town that had fewer pedestrians.

"Hey, it's a good thing your windows are tinted," I said cheerfully. "No one will be able to see me torture you." I hoped my genuine smile helped him to understand how his child victims must have felt. I didn't even care if he was incapable of experiencing empathy.

Of course, he tried to scream for help, but I wouldn't let him. When he finally gave up, I explained some things.

"I'm going to ask you a lot of questions. More will follow if you're still alive. I already know the answer to *some* of those questions. If you do not tell me the truth, I will cut off your oxygen supply until you lose consciousness. If I cut off your oxygen supply *too* long, and you accidentally die, I will pound your chest hard enough to leave terrible bruises on you, but hopefully, you will be resuscitated. However, truthfully, it may or may not revive you. You might, just, die. So, being honest is paramount in your efforts to stay alive."

Obscenities.

"Very good. Predictability always works in my favor. Let's get started, shall we? When you abduct a child, or coerce them into following you willingly, who do you sell them to?"

More obscenities flowed freely, so I focused on his neck and watched him struggle. His wide, horrified eyes bulged and his mouth flew open and quivered as he fought to get oxygen to his brain. Then he passed out.

I noticed a fresh, unread Wall Street Journal in the back seat and reached back to pick it up.

He probably never reads these, but still carries them around everywhere he goes to make himself feel intelligent.

For a moment, I considered opening it up to the stock market section to check on my investments, but didn't really have time for that. Instead, I rolled the paper up tight and slapped his face hard enough to leave red marks. He regained consciousness after a half-dozen swats.

"You did not tell me the truth, so I cut off your oxygen supply until you passed out, didn't I? Just like I said I would. That time, you did not die, but you *will* die if you don't tell me the truth. So, when you abduct a child, or coerce them into going with you willingly, who do you sell them to?"

He didn't last long. The guy was hard core until *he* was the one suffering. I got answers quickly, which I texted to Carla in real time.

We had our next target!

I paralyzed the child rapist/abductor one last time so I could drag him back into the driver's seat. Unfortunately, I took too long to get him settled. In his weakened state, he died from anoxia. I kept the promise to myself. He would never abuse another child. I removed the restraints and left his engine running to help confuse the coroner.

As I walked back to my car, I used my phone to check on those investments.

Next Rungs

Ascending the rungs of a well-organized crime network is a dangerous climb. I had to take significant risks. However, if I needed to abandon the plan and escape, having the ability to scorch the earth around me made the gamble easier to accept. It also helps to know that these particular criminals don't deserve to live, anyway. The drug dealers I had, literally, *focused* on in the past had all hurt children indirectly, which is bad enough, but targeting teens and younger children for sexual exploitation? There is nothing worse a human can do.

When you're taking out a crime organization one level at a time, working your way to the top, you have to move fast or the monsters at the top become aware and set traps for you. I'd been *there* before. I let that whiney dude in the black luxury car get the better of me about three years earlier, and I hadn't forgotten the lesson I had learned. I didn't hesitate to take the information I extracted from the law office worker and put it to use.

Carla helped. Just after lunch, I noticed her through the window of a van parked in the hotel's front entrance turnabout. She saw me, too, but we ignored each other. She had colleagues in there with her, with several more in other vehicles nearby. I went in through the front door and made my way to the bar.

The place was posh. My first thought was, *there is no way this hotel is part of an underage prostitution operation*. However, the unshaven and prison-tatted bartender looked rough, so I thought maybe the lead was legit. The only barstool taken was the third one from the end, but that was where I was supposed to sit. A clean-cut guy in a suit watched the ice cubes he was twirling in the bottom of his glass.

I walked back out into the hotel lobby, sat where I could see the third stool in a reflection, and waited. I picked up a magazine and read an entire article about how the treasure hunt on Oak Island was rewriting world history, and waited some more.

Eventually, the bartender handed the clean-cut guy a credit card and a receipt. I stayed put for a minute before taking my place in the seat so that I would not seem too enthusiastic. A moment before I stood, someone else got up from a table and moved to the third stool. The new customer whispered to the bartender, who poured something into a glass, handed it to him, and stepped away. At the other end of the bar, the barkeep picked up his phone and sent a text.

Again, several minutes passed before the bartender received another text. He then picked up what looked like a credit card wrapped in a receipt and handed them to the new customer, but the guy had not handed him a credit card, and he didn't pay for the drink. The new customer threw the rest of his drink down his throat and hurried to the elevator.

Those aren't credit cards. They're room keys.

I browsed that whole magazine while two more men went through the same routine. They were handed a room key wrapped in what looked like a receipt, and then they went to the elevators. Busy place, but when a woman went through the same routine, she didn't wait long. She was given a room key and went straight to the hotel without even tasting her drink.

A woman paying for underage sex? Seriously? I thought only we men could sink to this level of mental and moral degeneracy. She needs to go to prison, too.

Finally, no one took the last moron's place. I sat on the stool and when the bartender approached, I parroted what the law office worker had told me to say. "I'll have something fresh. Neat."

The rough bartender's demeanor changed for a brief moment. There appeared to be apprehension in his eyes. He did not reply, but nodded as he walked away.

He altered his response and he didn't pour me a drink. Something's wrong.

The bartender sent a text and received a reply almost immediately. He took his time coming back to my end of the bar, where he glanced at the exterior door and said, "Hey, don't I know you from the force? Are you still with NYPD, or did you get that job with the feds?"

Ha! He thinks that is a clever way of finding out if I'm a cop.

"Aw, hell no, I've never seen you before in my life, and if you want to know if I'm a cop, just ask, because, with all those prison tats, no one is ever going to believe you were a cop."

He laughed and asked point blank, "Are you in law enforcement at all?"

"*Hell*, no. I'm like, the exact opposite of a cop."

"Sorry, had to ask." Then he whispered, "You can either go to room four-twenty-three, or you can get the hell out of here."

If he wasn't part of the problem, I'd thank him for trying to help me.

To answer his question, I very deliberately got up and walked to the elevator. While I was out of sight, waiting on the elevator, I texted Carla as fast as I could.

The bartender is def involved, check his phone fast, but don't come upstairs yet

Carla knew things hadn't gone according to plan. Or at least not according to *her* plan.

PLEASE be careful! These people are ruthless

Duh. I'm glad she wasn't there to see me roll my eyes.

The door swung open before I had a chance to knock, and two thugs pointed guns at my chest. Behind the louts I could see someone at the desk, leaning back in his chair to supervise the encounter. Sadly, this kind of thing had happened to me so frequently that it had stopped bothering me. I just laughed. The door behind me also opened and I could *feel* another gun or two pointed at my back. Didn't change anything.

After a bit of a stalemate moment, I added a little cheer to my demeanor. "Hi, fellas! Should I come in, or are you going to beat me right here in the hall?"

I attempted to time things so that the two thugs' bodies hit the floor at the same time the door slammed. It didn't quite work out, but it was close. When I focused on the other guy's neck, he slid off of his chair and onto the rug with his legs bent awkwardly underneath him. I heard something pop. I'm pretty sure it was one of his knees.

Keeping him paralyzed to the best of my ability, I used a napkin from my pocket to pick up one of the thugs' guns and whacked both of them in the back of the head as hard as I could. One time each, because the first hit to the head rarely causes blood splatter, but subsequent ones do. However, with no heartbeat, there would be no blood flowing, so there would be nothing there to spray on the blows that followed, and I wanted the medical examiner to assume the blow to the head was the cause of death.

Hopefully, my identity would remain hidden. I did not want the wrong people to know I was back in New York.

Belts, phone cords, pillowcases and sheets make decent restraints when you don't have any cording. And a rolled-up, damp wash cloth makes a good gag when you don't want the hotel guests in the next room hearing screams. They have no way of knowing that the complaints are coming from someone who takes advantage of vulnerable girls so that he can turn them into underaged prostitutes. I wrapped a washcloth around the small bar of soap from the shower so I could shove the gag into his mouth without getting bitten.

And scream, he did. Or at least he tried. I didn't even ask him any questions at first. I dislocated his left shoulder and broke his right clavicle before I asked him anything, just to make sure he knew what kind of pain was coming.

I tried to look sad while I messed with his head. "Okay, I admit that I'm angry. For the past half hour, I have inflicted severe pain all over your body because I'm angry. I'm mad because you throw away the lives of children like it's *nothing*, so I'm forcing *you* to endure intense pain and anguish, like it's *nothing*."

Shaking his arm from side to side jiggled his broken clavicle so the fragmented ends of the bone ground together and scraped his pectoral and sternocleidomastoid muscles. He thrashed and shrieked into his soapy wash cloth. When he calmed down enough to open his eyes, I jerked his arm again, only I moved it up and down this time for maximum discomfort, until I noticed he had ruptured a couple of blood vessels in his face.

"Here's some advice. Cooperate. Tell me all about your organization, including the traps your idiots used to put me here."

Dude sang like a whale. He sounded a lot like a humpback too, as he experienced pain like he'd never even imagined. I rationalized that when someone sexually abuses hundreds of women and children, traumatizing them for life, then they should experience an equivalent amount of pain, only compressed into the short amount of time they have left to live.

Yeah. I was pissed.

And of course, after I extracted as much information from him as I could, there was only one thing left to do. I could not allow him to be reintroduced into society after being "rehabilitated" by a prison sentence. Nor did I want him to weasel his way out of a nice, long prison sentence because of some ridiculous technicality like being tortured, or because of a botched prosecution. I ended his wretched existence with the same mercy he allowed the children who entered his influence.

The job wasn't finished, though. There were the thugs across the hall to deal with and all the young sex slaves to free. Assuming they were open to being saved after being victims of severe psychological warfare. I opened the door and peeked out to get the room number across the hall, and then propped the door open with the latch lock. I called their room on the hotel phone. When one of them answered I used a loud whisper. "Get over here. *Now!*"

Two more thugs came running into the room. They froze when they saw their dead cohorts on the floor and me standing there looking all judgy. One went for his gun and the other turned to run, but both collapsed into their fate, never to abuse a child again. I bashed the back of their heads one time each, the same way I did the other two.

I called Carla and told her what I had learned. Mostly. There was no possible way I could get to *all* the people The Whale Singer named, so I held back information on the highest-ranking child abuser in their organization for myself. I'd deal with him personally. The rest of the people he had named would have to be arrested as soon as possible. But before that, the prostitutes in this fancy hotel needed to be rounded up and treated as victims, not criminals. I knew that Carla would see to them personally, so I took off to start my next task.

Yes, Ma'am!

From the inside of an unmarked van, Carla watched her lover walk into the hotel, but ignored him. She did not want the two uniforms and the IT tech with her to know that he was part of her plan. All four of them had on their heavy jackets, which made their bodies a little too warm, but left their hands free to get cold. One of the men did not smell great, but in the tight quarters, she did not know which one. Together, they waited. And waited.

Everyone's patience was being tried, but Carla finally got a text. As she stepped out of the back of the van she barked an order to her colleagues, who were starting to follow her. "Stay here, but be ready. I'll radio when I need you."

She also entered through the hotel lobby and looked around casually before heading for the bar, but the bartender "made" her immediately. He stopped his mindless cleaning and began easing his way towards the cash register and his phone, so Carla pulled her gun as fast as any gunslinger from the old west.

"FBI! Freeze!"

The guy didn't stop. He merely slowed a little. Behind her, she saw several single men and a couple get up and dash out of the bar, which distracted her for a moment. The bartender continued moving closer to his station with his hands up as though he had surrendered. She had to assume he wanted to dive down, grab his phone, and send a warning to his colleagues, but Carla knew not to let that happen.

"Move any closer to that phone and I will put four rounds in you *before* you hit the floor and *swear* I thought you were going for a gun."

For a moment, it looked like the guy considered suicide by proxy, so Carla added, "I'll only shoot arms and legs then. I promise that you *will* live to see prison, either full of holes or healthy enough to defend yourself once you're there."

His tough-guy persona faded away as he sighed. Carla reached over the counter to retrieve his phone and pocketed it, then radioed the cops outside. When they had him cuffed and out from behind the bar, she used his finger to unlock his phone, and then again to change the PIN so it could be easily accessed.

"I'm done. Take him away, and do not let him talk to anyone. *Any*one. Not until we get his superiors."

"Yes, ma'am."

Under her breath, she added, "If he was brutalized to the point where he couldn't communicate for days…"

"Yes, ma'am."

"Oh, sorry. I may have spoken a private thought."

"Yes, ma'am."

Carla didn't clarify if she meant it or not, and the cops, both loving fathers of daughters, didn't ask. She also managed to keep her thoughts about being called 'ma'am' to herself, and didn't waste a second getting the bartender's phone to the tech guy in the van. She then called for the backup officers and social workers who were standing by, giving them the list of rooms from the texts the bartender had received, where they would likely find prostitutes who were mostly child sex slaves.

"Treat them *all* the same way you would a victim of rape."

The IT Geek in the van went to work on the phone the second he laid hands on it, and had answers within a couple of minutes. However, there was not much information on the phone, which was fairly new.

"I'm sorry, Agent Bright, there's just not a lot on here. The suspect had a few numbers he called, or that contacted him, mostly typical personal calls like pizza delivery and such, but there was one number he texted several times per day. I already have the office working on tracking that."

"Okay, keep looking. Keep digging."

"Ummm, well, there's nothing left to check."

Agent Bright's tone was forceful but respectful. "Then just *act* like you're still looking. Tell me you understand."

The tech wondered why she was so stressed, but just cleared his throat and responded, "Yes, ma'am."

She managed to keep her thoughts and her eye rolls to herself again. The tech changed the type of connection he used, reestablished the link, and performed his routine searches again, but did not discover anything new.

"Um, what are we waiting for?"

Carla shot him a look that nearly knocked him off his stool, so he looked in the system folders again to see if any files were hidden there. He opened every image on the phone to make sure someone had not hidden a data file by saving it with a graphics extension, even though his scan had already verified that the files were images.

Finally, Agent Bright's phone rang. "Anything?" She paused, then her eyes widened. "Yeah?" She pointed at the tech, "Write this down."

The tech readied his pen and began scribbling notes from an unknown caller. From the notes he was taking, he realized it was information they could use to infiltrate higher rungs of the child sex ring. The IT Geek was a family man as well, which was *also* part of her plan.

Pointing to the notes he'd written, then to the phone he was working on, Carla asked point blank, "How fast can you make *that* information appear to have come from *that* phone?"

The tech's face was blank for a moment as he considered that. "Fast."

"Good man." He had earned the privilege of not being chewed out for calling her "ma'am."

That evening, several teams took down dozens of suspects who were previously unapproachable, including the Philly miscreant I regretted leaving alive. Warrants to search homes, computers and phones were instrumental in gathering the evidence to put them all behind bars for a long time.

Their *own* homes and families might be the last ones they'd ever destroy.

Three! Two?!

I pressed a short piece of surgical tape over the peephole and tried the doorknob, being careful not to make any noise that might alert the lowlife inside. It was locked, of course, but I had to try. However, I peered into the crack of the door and could see that the deadbolt was not engaged.

The basketball game he had on TV would help cover my entrance. Reaching into my pocket and looking over my shoulder down the hall of dingy doorways, I pulled out my pocketknife and forced the utility blade behind the old latch. It slid in effortlessly and I eased the latch out of the strike plate. As easy as that, I opened the locked door.

I always wanted to try that.

My instincts were screaming at me to engage a flight response. An increased heart rate and heavier breathing supported the notion, but my mind overruled good sense. Stealthy and slow, I opened the door and peeked in so that I could see what I was getting myself into.

The door opened up directly into the living room, via a short entryway, with the door to the kitchen to my right. I saw the arm of my child-abusing target in a recliner. His back was to me, thankfully. I slipped in and eased the door closed behind me. The latch clicked a little as it slipped back into place, but the TV noise drowned out the sound as someone scored a three-pointer, but *four* rejoicing arms pumped fists as *two* men yelled.

Aw, hell. Nothing ever seems to go according to plan.

My mind raced. Which one is the target, and more importantly, is the other one involved or just an old college pal over watching a game?

If one of these guys has nothing to do with the child sex ring, what do I do? I can't torture or kill someone only to find out they were not involved. I have to get out of here.

I reached behind me to open the door, but of course, I couldn't turn the doorknob because it was still locked. I fumbled around, looking for the mechanism, but did not dare take my eyes off the two guys. I finally found the ridged knob in the middle of the handle and tried to turn it.

Any second now, a commercial could come on and they'd jump up for another drink or snack or something.

The locking mechanism finally cooperated and turned. Still reaching around behind my back, I twisted the doorknob slowly. It squeaked. I froze, expecting them to turn around to investigate.

Thankfully, their focus remained on the game. I turned the doorknob more and felt the door move free. For fear of that commercial I knew was coming, I slipped out quickly. I thought about reaching back around and resetting the lock to leave it exactly as I found it, but did not want the latch to click again. With the stealth of a parent closing the bedroom door of a napping baby, I pulled it closed and eased the latch back into place.

When I was three steps away, I heard a commercial come on and I imagined them racing each other to the fridge.

I either needed a new plan, or I needed to delay my poorly thought-out current plan. Outside on the busy Brooklyn streets, the nighttime air had a penetrating chill to it. My bargain burner was barely smart enough to allow me to log on to their game's website, but at least I could see enough to know when to try to go back. There was nothing within walking distance that was open, so there was nothing to do but hang out or go for a stroll.

I'm getting my steps in tonight.

With two minutes left in the game, I headed back. Standing by the window at the opposite end of the hall, I held my phone to my ear and watched my target's door. I waited so long that I wondered if he had already left. It was a long time to fake a phone call. My arm was getting tired from holding the phone and my feet hurt from standing and walking all evening.

"We'll get 'em next time!"

Finally.

Both of them were huge, mountain-sized men.

Glad I don't have to wrestle them.

The guy was younger than I expected. Someone so high up in an organization is usually older, after having to earn their way into positions of authority. He was likely the son or nephew of someone powerful.

That old idiom is true though. The bigger they are, the harder they fall. I had a hell of a time getting that guy back into his recliner. I wanted it to appear as though he had died in his sleep, so when I got the contact information for the next rung in the ladder, I left the TV and lights on, and locked the door on the way out.

I used a secure instant message app to contact Carla so that no one on the subway would hear my conversation.

Carla- The next rung on the ladder is not a person, but rather the act of logging onto their network. I'm going to need a phone that the FBI can monitor and take over.

i knew u were holding out

I wasn't holding out, I was doing my part. (-
` ,

uh-huh. how fast do you need it and where are u

I'm hoping to access their network in the morning, before they realize we've been taking out the rungs below them, but I'd like to get a little sleep first... on the subway now, on the way home.

of course, i'll make sure they have a phone ready for u when we wake up COME HOME

Thanks. Exhausted. OMW ♡

cool! how'd u do that?

What, the heart?

yes

C'mon, now, you know those kinds of things are IT Geek secrets... like magicians who never reveal their magic tricks.

really? sorry

No, Babe, I was just joking. It's not a secret, it's ASCII. You know we IT Geeks ♡ to share. If you're on your laptop, just hold down the

Alt key and press 9825 on your number keypad. (Has to be on the keypad part of your keyboard.)

♡

Yay! Very good.

♡

♡♡♡

♡

Oh, good grief.

Love you too, Babe.

I ♡ u 2

!

i'd make a good nerd, huh?

Sigh. I keep telling you, we prefer 'IT Geek' ...ah-ight?

♡♡♡

My stop's coming up. I'll be home soon.

⊜

oops! ♡

She makes me chuckle.

A Chip Off the Old Anonymity

Carla was already gone when a particularly disturbing dream woke me. It wasn't what you'd call a nightmare, but troubling enough to take a few minutes to shake off. My guilt had infiltrated my subconscious and manifested itself as a bad dream. I'd taken a lot of lives in the past few years, very few of which I regret, but if I could go back in time, I'd change the way I handled the prison riot in Texas.

I've often wondered if I had taken the life of someone who had been wrongly imprisoned. Yes, they had been given a few *days* to turn themselves in and surrender, as several had, so if any of the innocent ones were still actively rioting in the prison, they had put themselves in harm's way.

Still, I had regrets. And my subconscious had exploited that guilt. I jumped in the shower, washing the agonizing dream and its residual thoughts down the drain.

A note from Carla helped get me out of my funk. She left it by the coffee machine where she knew I'd find it. The pot was half full and still hot, so I poured myself a tall one. Her note said she had gone to pick up the traceable phone I needed, and that she'd be back by 9:00 or so. At the bottom of the note, she wrote "I ALT+9825 u!"

I chuckled again. *She gets me.*

Shortly before nine she showed up briefly with a fairly new phone.

"It was used in a couple of undercover operations, so it has some history in case they check the phone closely. Use the name Bill Butler so the history can remain intact."

"Good thinking. What did you tell them it was for?"

"Well, Ken has stopped asking questions because, A, he knows I won't answer, and, two—"

Not quite believing she had already forgotten that she had started with "A" I kept quiet and let her go on.

"...I'm sure he knows I'm working with someone who may not be legit, and—"

I raised an eyebrow in anticipation of whether she would finish with "C" or "three."

"...finally, I think he wants these child abusers even more than we do."

Made me laugh. But it was nervous laughter. "Okay, that would have been funnier had it not been used in such a grim context."

Carla grinned. "You get me."

Remembering my *she-gets-me* thought a few minutes earlier made me happy. "Yeah. Apparently so."

She switched gears. "What's the plan? How are you going to get on their network?"

I considered that for a second to think of a way to sum up the complicated process quickly, but then thought of something to say that would probably prevent me from having to explain. "Do you know what a public formula 64UID is?"

"A wha—um, no."

"It's a time-sensitive, sixty-four-character Unicode identifier that reduces to zero when you apply a specific formula to it, and it ceases to be valid after eight minutes. It's far better than a UUID or a GUID."

Carla had that look. "Like I know what *those* are."

"More details? Like, there are hundreds of websites that provide them, but you have to know whi– "

"No. No more details, please. Like I said before, just handle it. I need to get back anyway. We still have some follow-up on all that information you got for us yesterday."

"Okay, cool."

"Thanks again for that. And, by the way, I could tell Ken was grateful, but he supported your anonymity by saying nothing."

"The feeling is mutual. The guy seems alright." *But I'm not ready to try to earn the trust of another person whose job it is to put me in prison.*

We went our separate ways for the day, which I always hated because it reminded me of Turkmenistan. She went back to work and I jumped on the subway to go to the mall off of Columbus Circle. As I approached the entrance, I couldn't help but look into Central Park and think about when I first discovered my ability to disrupt the nervous system of many other life forms.

Being there again made me wonder what became of the thugs who got away with their lives that night. Had our paths ever crossed again? Or did they learn their lesson and go on to become useful members of society? I also thought about what might have happened to the kid's gun that I tossed into the mailbox.

Ugh. I hope my author friend doesn't try to turn this moment into some kind of full circle thing.

I didn't linger long. I had a simple but daunting task to accomplish and wanted to get to it. I went into the mall and tried to blend in.

Because it was a cold and sunny day, I fit right in with my cap and sunglasses. The crowds and the free, heavily-used Wi-Fi would make it difficult for anyone to find me, but easy for the FBI to track which IP addresses I accessed.

A dark roast was brewing in a deli and smelled too good to pass by. I indulged, sitting in their section on the empty end of a long, community picnic table. I settled in next to the wall so I could have a little privacy. I logged onto the free Wi-Fi and began generating a new formula 64UID. When a woman sat across the table from me, I nodded and spoke some friendly greeting. She rolled her eyes, got up, and sat at the next table where fellow New Yorkers knew to ignore her. I laughed on the inside.

I checked the 64UID to make sure the applied formula generated zero. It did, so I used my other phone to text Carla.

```
I'm ready to access their website, are your
peeps ready?
```

```
yes
```

I typed the relatively simple URL into the phone's browser.

Here we go.

<Enter>

The website looked clean and polished. It was professionally done.

I hope they stole that code, or tricked some poor sap into writing it. I'd hate it if real IT Geeks are helping to maintain this organization.

The page had a typical login screen with the Forgot Password and Create New Login links, but it also had an option for entering a code.

I'm betting that's for the 64UID.

Copy and paste entered the code without errors. The website chugged along and displayed a spinning icon while it applied the formula to the 64UID. Another screen popped up requiring the MAC address of the device I was using, but it had a timer that started at sixty-four seconds. I scrambled through the settings of the unfamiliar phone as I counted the seconds off in my head as best as I could.

Twenty... Security? Privacy? System! Thirty. Ugh, not System. About? Yes! Thirty-five. Oh, Wi-Fi MAC or Device MAC? Uhhhh, device! Highlight and copy... find my other window... where is it? Forty-five. There! Scroll back down... Paste, fifty, tap Submit, more chugging. Whew! Nine seconds left. Plenty of time.

The website loaded an extensive menu page while the hourglass icon rolled over and over, so I sent Carla another text from my other phone.

```
I'm in, I think.

I know, we can see your screen. u cut that
close, babe

Please. PLENTY of time left.
```

I realized how inappropriately jovial everyone was as I accessed some of the pages on that website. It was horrendous. I gagged. Not just once, but several times. Some of the "children" were just toddlers. Three or four years old, but most of the videos seemed to focus on young girls just reaching puberty.

Rage swept over me. My face was hot and my fingers ran cold. I wanted to kill everyone involved. I *needed* to end their pathetic lives in the most unbearable ways I could imagine, but I could not even look at the screen to access the links. I knew I needed to stay online and simulate some pervert looking at the photos and watching the videos, but I just couldn't.

Can't do this. I'm sorry but I can't do this anymore.

This is Agent Ken Starnes, Agent Bright is currently indisposed. We understand your reluctance, as some of us are having the same issues. Im going to send something to our phone. Just click ok and well take over.

The other phone chimed and a popup was asking for permission to control the phone remotely. Relieved, I pressed the OK button.

Thank you.

I placed the FBI's phone face down on the table and did my best to get the deplorable, unsettling images out of my head.

Can you please text me when you're finished?

Yes, but it will be a while. An hour, maybe more.

That's ok. I'm here as long ss you need me.

Staying put seemed like the thing to do, to reduce the chances of moving into a Wi-Fi dead zone and losing the connection. I tried to think about the beautiful Canadian landscape where I had hiked, and the fascinating cenotes I had seen in Mexico. But not even the memories of the raw beauty of the Rocky Mountains around my old cabin could shake loose the images of children being sexually abused. I felt like the very core of who I was had been changed forever.

More pressing issues got my mind off the atrocities. A man in a suit with a bulge under his left arm was scanning everyone in the mall. I texted Carla and/or Ken.

```
Did you send someone here to look for me?

no, why? I'm back, btw, sorry, I totally lost
it.

There is someone who looks like a fed looking
around at everyone.

its not us, get out of there! now! i will see
what i can find out

I'm leaving, but hiding t phone here so u csn
continue.
```

I knew I was typing too fast and making mistakes but I didn't care. They understood. As quickly and inconspicuously as possible, I wiped down the phone with paper napkins and then wrapped the phone in several more. I gulped down the last bit of cold coffee and stuffed the phone into the empty cup as I walked to the plastic trash bins. I dropped the FBI's phone in, hoping that the connection would not be lost. Then I headed for the exit while texting Carla.

```
Do you still have the connection/

yes

I have to walk by this guy to get to the exit

He's not one of us but could still be a federal
agent, dont hurt him

Hadn't planned to. I'll let you know when I'm
out.
```

I took my time as I walked past the suit, with my eyes glued to my phone like most people. When I was near him, I switched to the camera, pointed it in his direction, and used the burst feature to capture thirty or forty images of the guy through heavy pedestrian traffic. Hopefully, at least one would be clear.

At the bottom of the subway stairs across the street from the mall, I stopped and turned around to see if he had followed me. Apparently not.

I'm out, and I don't think I'm being followed. I'm sending you a few photos of him. See if you can ID him?

ok, i will. listen, i know this is prob a bad time to bring this up, but, ken read our previous text messages while i was in the bathroom puking, including the ones where i call you "Babe"

Ugh

ill let you know what becomes of it, for now, just get the hell away from there

Who *Are* You?

Carla and Ken, along with several other dedicated FBI agents, pounded on keyboards and shouted into phones. The scramble was on to find as many of the losers that were on the child porn website as they could, and get local law enforcement to watch them until arrest warrants could be issued. They were already coordinating a plan to arrest as many of them as they could at the same time.

Everyone was so busy that only Ken noticed Carla was avoiding him. When he caught her off by herself, he approached her and asked, "You know we need to talk about this, right?"

She sighed. "Yes."

"Your personal life is none of my business, of course, but how did he… or she, I don't know, get involved in this case?"

In mid-sentence, Carla gave Ken a glare. In a sarcastic tone, she mocked him. "Oh, you want to talk about *that*? I thought you meant you wanted to talk about you invading my privacy."

Ken's "Really?" face made her wish she hadn't lit into her trusted co-worker like that, but she was still ticked off about it.

"Carla, when you handed me your phone—"

"Yes, I handed you my phone when I abandoned my post to go puke. I remember." She was getting angrier by the moment and couldn't stop spiraling.

"Okaaaaay. Who *are* you? Look, all I intended to do was answer 'Babe's' text." It was Ken's turn to be a little sarcastic. "But right there on the screen that *you handed me*, you called this person

'Babe.' I didn't go scrolling through your messages looking for trouble. It was right there."

She realized he was right and calmed down. Disappointed in herself, she sat on a desk, and Ken, being Ken, made a suggestion. "How about if we forget the past few moments of this conversation and start over? Yeah?"

"You're too kind."

"I have genuine and sincere concerns about his, or her, well-being—"

"*His*, okay?" She was surprised to learn that Ken knew so little about her personal life.

"*His* well-being. We are mixing with some dangerous people who have *no* morals."

"I know this."

"Is he in law enforcement? Or just an informant? And if he's 'just' an informant, how does he know enough about these vile people to get us all this information and, more importantly, how do *you* know *him*?"

Carla realized he hadn't put two and two together yet. Ken had not yet figured out that "Babe" was also the serial killer they had nearly arrested almost a year ago.

"Okay, those are all legit concerns and questions. And I agree that you really should know more. However, I already talked to *Babe*—" Carla shot him a sideways glance. "—about it, but he is not yet willing to extend trust to another tier. 'Yet' being the key word here. I can assure you that he is not involved with this organization at all other than to infiltrate and see them all brought to justice."

"Did he kill the perps in the hotel room?"

"He's one man. One average-sized man. How could he kill a roomful of thugs with guns?" Carla felt better about asking misleading questions than she did about outright lying.

Both stood in silence for a moment, looking anywhere but into each other's eyes.

"Ken, I'm sorry I was snippy."

"Already forgotten." He nodded towards the rest of the team, who were all a little louder than usual, but few of them were actually working together. Most of them seemed to be avoiding each other. "Those photos have us all upset."

"There were hundreds of children in those files. *Hundreds*."

"We're going to get these bastards. Tell your informant he has my full support in whatever he needs and in his anonymity. But *damn* it, Carla, I am *not* going to call him Babe." He used his elbow to nudge her.

A small burst of laughter helped ease the tension.

Ken pulled a piece of paper from his back pocket. Unfolding it revealed a photo of the mysterious man in the mall. "Let's talk about this guy. Is he a fed? Or is he some kind of security for this ring? Or was he just some guy at the mall?"

Carla took the photo and gave it a long, hard look. "Who *are* you?"

Patience of an Ambush Predator

Qian sat in his idling car and waited. Wispy trails of condensation followed each vehicle while brilliant morning sunlight streaming between tall, New York buildings gave him an excuse to hide behind his sun visor. Some days he could parallel park in the street close enough to the exit of *Special* Agent Bright's parking garage to see the faces of the drivers. Other times he would have to wait down the street, and could only see the people who exited and turned in his direction.

He had followed her six times since his last encounter with Sciens. There were three other mornings when he had seen her, but was unable to tail her. He hadn't seen the focus of all his loathing since that day he had nearly run him over in his stolen, luxury SUV. The only reason Agent Bright was still alive was so that she could lead him to Sciens again, but she hadn't, so she was losing her usefulness.

When he saw Agent Bright pull out of the darkened garage exit, he decided to kill her if the opportunity presented itself, just to make Sciens suffer. With a childish smirk on display for all the people he imagined were watching him, Qian pulled into traffic, three cars behind Carla.

Take Him Out or In?

The morning was so wintry that even the floors in Carla's apartment were cold. Just for fun, while she was in the shower, I tossed a big bath towel in the dryer. When I heard her turn the water off, I pulled the towel out and ran into the bathroom. She was reaching for a towel, so I said, "Wait!" Probably a little too enthusiastically, but she didn't mind when I wrapped that warm towel around her. She stood there for several seconds with her eyes closed and a goofy little smile on her face.

Dressed and ready to go, Carla peered out of her fourth-story window and noticed a certain car parked on the street. She had also noticed the same car on other mornings, always parked where the driver could see the exit of her parking garage. On cold mornings like this, she could see that the engine was running.

That's three times in the past four days.

Undeterred, she hurried downstairs to her car and pulled out into heavy traffic. A dozen miles later, in The Bronx, the car was still behind her.

"Hmmm. I didn't lose him in traffic this time."

She took the Bartow Circle exit into Pelham Bay Park and turned down a beautiful stretch of quiet, tree-lined road, where she predicted the man would make his move. There were good reasons why her FBI title was *Special* Agent.

"Reeeaaadyyy... Here he coooooomes up on the leeeft. Now!"

I sat up in the rear seat and did my best to focus on the driver's chest. I thought I had focused correctly, but his car slammed into ours and knocked me back down onto the seat. Carla stomped on the brakes. As we came to a screeching halt, I rolled into the floorboard face first. I managed to scramble up and get out of the car at the same time as Carla, who had to secure the vehicle and unbuckle.

The other car had bounced off of us and smashed into a tree. Steam was spewing from the radiator and the airbag had deployed. Carla aimed her gun in the general direction of the driver, who was fighting to get the dusty airbag out of his face.

While we eased closer to the wreck, Carla yelled something typical. "FBI! Slowly put your hands where I can see them!" But I thought, *Screw that. There is no way this guy is taking orders from a woman. Or from someone older than him. Or any*one. I focused on his neck for a split second, which was long enough to cause him to drop anything in his hand, but not long enough for his head to fall into the field of focus. I moved around behind Carla to the driver's side and focused on his neck again.

Together, we peeked through the driver's side window. Sure enough, there was a freaking hand cannon in the seat next to him and a sawed-off shotgun in the passenger side floorboard. I released my focus on him when Carla moved in closer so that she did not walk into my line of fire. He needed to breathe anyway. She tried the door, but it was locked. I saw her switch on the safety of her heavy 9mm and was surprised when she swung it like a club to smash through the window with a single, forceful blow.

With the gun's safety back off, she pointed it at his face as she reached in with her other hand to unlock and open the door. Carla brazenly reached in to unbuckle him. I wanted to paralyze him again so that he couldn't surprise her, but could not do so without endangering her. All I could do was stay out of the way and watch.

She pulled him out of the car away from the weapons and shoved him face-down into the grass. A knee on his neck held him securely while she cuffed him, and I breathed a sigh of relief.

A thorough search revealed another gun in an ankle holster, and when she took it from him, he went crazy. Yelling and kicking, he tried to get up off the ground and made vile threats, so I focused on his neck for a few seconds again to shut him up.

She pulled the radio from her hip but I stopped her.

"Wait. What would they charge him with? Reckless driving? If you arrest him, he will be out of jail someday. It might be years from now, or maybe later today, but he'll be free and hunting for us, probably even madder than he is now."

Qian began yelling and screaming again, but this time it was more about calling for help than revenge. I focused on his neck again to silence him.

She hesitated and I added, "Or maybe he gets out soon because of a botched trial or intimidated jury."

"He's already in a wreck, here. No one would think twice if I took him out now."

"So, what? Just take his guns and leave him here dead?"

I'd never really talked about murdering someone in cold blood before. I had killed hundreds of people who were out to harm others, but this guy was contained. *Likely* on his way to jail for a long time although that was not guaranteed. I sighed and Carla seemed to know what I was thinking.

"I'm willing to take my chances with the system, but I also understand that you're at risk, too."

Kill him or arrest him? They both seemed like mistakes. Had I known in Turkmenistan what I know now...

Turning loose of Qian's neck, I allowed him to breathe. His body convulsed as he sucked in full breaths of air. I didn't care, but I noticed he had a chilling, haunted look in his eyes that did not quite match the situation he was in. Still half choking and desperate for enough oxygen, he managed to spit his thoughts into words. "You *destroyed* my entire *life*."

Leaning in close, I got right in his face, looked him in the eye, and forcefully whispered, "You son of a bitch. *They* attacked *me*. Your *colleagues* invited me there, but then tried to kill me when they realized they couldn't exploit me. I defended myself. This stops here and now. One way or the other, your bullshit stops. I may or may not allow you to live, but either way, this stops now."

I cut off his oxygen supply until I saw fear in his eyes. "Every precious breath of air you take for the rest of your miserable life, you owe to me. If I even *think* you're still planning revenge, I'll find a way to get to you and kill you in your jail cell."

With that, I walked down to the bike path along the beach. Just in time, too. Carla had several off-duty cops there, fast. Apparently, there was an NYPD shooting range school less than a mile away.

Special Agent Carla Bright. Impressive.

Qian must have sworn an oath of silence to himself. He didn't speak another word to Carla, or utter a single word to the arresting officers. He wouldn't even speak to his appointed attorney. He was, indeed, charged with reckless driving but also endangering the life of a law enforcement officer, evading arrest, carrying unregistered, concealed weapons, and possession of an illegal firearm.

Hopefully, he'll be in prison long enough to mature into a rationally thinking adult.

Carla's Folder, Ken's Task

Ken slipped into Carla's office and sat down. She stopped typing and looked at him, but he just stared back.

"You have that good-news-bad-news look about you."

The tiniest hint of shock swept Ken's face for a split second. "You know me too well, Carla. The good news first."

"Let's hear it."

"Thanks to, um, your *informant*, we have tracked down the Syrian." Ken was trying hard not to call the informant "Babe."

"That *is* good news. And the bad news? He slipped away again?"

"No. No, we haven't moved on him yet. We have him under surveillance to reduce the chances of him disappearing again. The bad news is, we still don't have enough direct evidence to arrest him."

"Well, on the bright side, maybe this time we have an ace in the hole." Carla looked lost in thought for a few moments. She knew *this* was the opportunity she had been waiting for.

Ken gave her a sideways look. "What are you thinking?"

"I'm pretty sure my *informant*," she looked at Ken and paused after she said "informant," knowing this was going to be a thing now, "can get to him, but…" Carla hesitated.

"Okay, I was hoping you'd say that, but, what?"

"He'll want some things in trade before he deals with that dangerous bastard."

Carla paused again and looked at Ken as though she were about to say something she would regret.

"What? Spit it out."

"You're probably not going to like it."

"I'm willing to trade just about anything to stop this child exploitation machine so, just name it."

She took a deep breath and plunged right in. "He's going to want to be in the witness protection program and—"

"Done."

"And immunity for any crimes he'll commit getting to the Syrian, and any crimes he may have committed leading up to this point."

"You're right."

"About what?" She was a little confused.

"I don't like it. This is a tough one. I'm on board, I think, as long he's not a part of the very problem we're fighting here or guilty of abusing children in any way."

"Oh, absolutely not. Just the opposite. He may have committed crimes finding out the information he gave us about this case, and while working towards similar situations in the past, but it was always to *stop* people from hurting children. I'd describe his efforts to protect kids as," Carla paused for a moment to choose the right word, "...fierce."

"Okay. Well, we'll have to go higher up on this one, but you have my support."

"And—"

"What? '*And*'? Seriously?"

"*And*, there is one more thing, but he wants this agreement in place before that's revealed."

Ken made an incredulous face. "How is that even possible?"

"We write up the agreement, make it official, and then he'll let us know what his last requirement is. I believe it is *nothing* compared to what he's already asking. If we are okay with it, we add whatever it is and work with him to get the Syrian. If we don't agree to these terms, we still have to find some other way to get to the Syrian, and you know better than anyone what that's been like. We've nothing to lose by trying this."

He felt like he needed to know more. "Tell me, do you know what this other thing is?"

"My informant assures me that the additional request is nothing we would hesitate to agree to, if the task is even possible. This last-minute condition is about him remaining anonymous until he is granted immunity."

"I understand. How fast do you think we can move on this?"

Carla sighed with relief. "Faster than we can make the agreement official, likely. He's already scheming his way in as we speak, so let's do our part and get busy with this."

"Oh. Okay. Well, it might take days to get all this typed up correctly and—"

She had opened her desk drawer and retrieved a folder. "All it needs is an approval."

"I see. And I'm betting you want *me* to get it approved."

A devilish little smile made Ken laugh. He took the folder and headed upstairs immediately, but wondered who really ran the department.

Egos and Solutions

Ken was having trouble getting his superiors to agree to my requests. Despite a crippling increase in heroin addictions and overdoses, and a rash of new disappearances by young "runaways," the ones in charge would rather pursue unknown charges against me than try to end the sexual exploitation of countless children and teens. Carla and I talked that afternoon.

"Maybe you and Ken have found the inside man who is in bed with the Syrian."

She considered the possibility but shook her head. "No, our boss couldn't be high enough up. He just hates doing anything that was not his idea. And he is simply immovable once he digs in his heels."

"In the corporate world, when I encountered egos like that, I would contact ego-boy's boss. I'd explain that even though I had a good boss that I was happy with, I needed a little help implementing something. Occasionally, when I was feeling especially passive-aggressive, I'd throw in something like being afraid my boss felt the difficult decision was above his pay grade."

Carla laughed but punted it back. "That won't work in this structure, at least not coming from me, but if the email came from *you*…"

"I'm on it. What are their emails? It's best to cc everyone."

She laughed again. "You're like that video of the monkey pulling the tiger's ears."

"Come on, let's walk down the street and find some free Wi-Fi. I sure don't want to send it from yours."

"Okay. I could use a spicy chai."

The email produced results from her boss's boss even faster than it did in the corporate world. But of course, there was a catch. He tried to be tough in his email.

Show me a video with enough evidence to arrest and convict The Syrian, and I will agree to your demands.

I rolled my eyes but replied in a respectful font.

First, Assistant Director Jaris, I have **requests**, not demands. I'm hoping to work **with** the FBI, not **against** your esteemed colleagues. Here is how I need this to work: I will show the video to agents Starnes and Bright, then immediately delete it. When I get my agreement, and I'm safely into the witness protection plan with my new identity, I'll provide a quality copy of the video to the FBI, so you can finally stop this guy.

He answered within a couple of minutes.

Agreed, but we will require a complete list of everything for which you need immunity.

I rolled my eyes again. Creating a list like that would be somewhere between extremely long and impossible to provide. Even if I gave it an honest effort, there is no way I could remember everything.

That's not going to work for me. If I forget something, or get some technicality wrong, someone will "throw the book at me" to make up for other crimes I have immunity for. It has to be all or nothing. I need a blank slate and a fresh start.

His quick reply told me he had just been fishing for information.

Fine, but as I stated, your video must lead to an arrest and conviction of this Syrian criminal. Now what is this other stipulation you want added to the agreement? I'll add it right now.

I thought about making him wait until the last moment to add it, as I had planned, but he seemed amiable and willing to give until it hurt so that they could catch an exceptionally evasive criminal. I tried to word the "stipulation" so that it was perfectly accurate, yet a little misleading. I was hoping that when I said "property," he'd think I meant that I wanted a few small items returned instead of my cabin in the Rocky Mountains.

Any cash confiscated, or any confiscated property that still exists, that was taken from me and/or my employees, at any time in the past, will be returned, no questions asked. It's a short list, but the items on it are very important to me.

My request was clear, but he seemed to think it was murky.

We can't return stolen money or merchandise, or any other objects that are illegal or harmful, under any circumstances.

I thought I had better try to reassure him, but still did not want to reveal too much.

Nothing I need returned is illegal, or stolen, or harmful in any way. It's something most people have, but still, make sure the agreement says "no questions asked." I just want my property, my legal property, returned to me and my employees.

We did not have to wait long for any of his previous replies, but this one took longer.

I've added the stipulation.

Thank you! I'll have this video within a few days, so please have this agreement prepared soon, and ready for all of us to sign.

After another pause in the email conversation, he requested more information.

I added another stipulation to the agreement. The video must lead to an arrest and conviction. I also need to know your name and Social Security number.

The new stipulation seemed reasonable.

That's fine. We both want the same thing. And, leave the places for the name and SSN blank. I'll write that information in when the time comes.

Fair enough. Let Agent Starnes know if you need any support. Let's work together to get this criminal.

Thank you, Mr. Jaris.

About a half hour later, I received an email with the signed agreement attached. I read it thoroughly to make sure there was no ambiguous legalese, and that was that. I was on a path to get my life back. I thanked my girlfriend repeatedly and showered her with praise and admiration. I'm pretty sure the badass Carla cried a little. The possibility of a normal life brought both of us joy.

The American Dream

Nurmuhammet Mammetgeldiyev, better known as "Dunlap" to some, stepped off a plane at JFK International Airport with a work permit in his hand and the American dream on his mind. But he was surprised to soon find himself in a large cage they called a "holding cell" with other immigrants. Strong body odor and old, dried urine assailed his nostrils.

Every day that passed deflated his optimism. Still, he remained strong, never once giving up hope, even though he endured *three weeks* of this humiliation.

Back in Turkmenistan, it had taken months to get the U.S. work permit, which cost him a third of the money Sciens had left him. Almost all the cash he spent went to well-placed bribes, so Dunlap did not understand why his entry into America had to be processed again. He remained patient, even though living conditions were deplorable, scuffles between detainees were common, and the food was bad.

Only one other person in the holding cell spoke Turkmen, his native language, and that was a man from Afghanistan. They stayed close and shared their hopes and dreams with each other until the Afghan was denied access and sent home.

When Dunlap was finally accepted into the United States of America, he rejoiced and openly wept joyous tears. And sorrowful tears, too, when he remembered that his grandmother's dying wish was for him to make it to America.

Dunlap was genuinely surprised when his belongings were returned to him and all his money was still rolled up in the pocket of an old pair of pants. But despite having all that cash returned to him, he still took the advice of the Afghan and checked into the cheapest weekly rate "hotel" he could find.

That weekend he found a minimum wage job in a restaurant, which was a lot more money than he was used to. When he saw the chefs working and creating beautiful dinner plates, he knew that was something he could do, and a new American dream was born.

I wonder where Sciens is and what he's doing right now. I wish I could thank him for this.

Well, Okay Then

I watched Carla wake up as soft, spring sunlight highlighted her neck and shoulder. When her eyes opened, she focused on me and smiled. Oh! That smile.

"Good morning."

She put her hand over her mouth. "Eeww! I need to brush my teeth."

I laughed as she kicked her way out from under the covers. Her tiny bathroom was not much bigger than the one in that RV and the single sink had us taking turns spitting. The warm aroma of coffee brewing pleased us both as we smeared cream cheese on toasted bagels. In the mornings, we often sat at a tiny round table in her breakfast nook. The windows overlooked a park on the other side of a busy street. Sometimes we'd make up stories about the people who passed by. But not today. Another conversation was on the agenda.

A heavy sigh set the mood for the subject on both our minds. "Okay, after weeks of planning, it's almost time to get this guy."

"I'll have an entire team made up of FBI and NYPD in place tomorrow. Remember, if things go south while you're in there, try to text '911' to me."

"I appreciate that."

"We checked and double-checked. No one knows anyone who might be there working undercover."

"Good to know."

Carla's face brightened, "By the way, not only did they add credit card fraud to the list of charges against Qian, INTERPOL has gotten involved. They want to extradite him to Lithuania for killing two unidentified people in a bar."

"Hmmm. Do two Lithuanian murders outweigh all the American charges?"

Carla shook her head. "If he were American, no. But he is from China, so we have to give him up."

"I don't like the sound of that. Should we have taken him out when we had the chance?"

"My guess is, doing time in Lithuania is going to be far worse than doing time in an American prison."

There was more to it than that, for me. "True, but if he is over there, I can't make good on my threat."

"Don't be so sure." Carla punctuated her sentence, and breakfast, with a wink.

Later, after a shower, we decided to get out and enjoy the beautiful spring day and take some time to relax before we put tomorrow's plan in motion. When Carla was ready, she walked into the living room, stopped and stood there, pecking on her phone. I sat and watched, ogling her and thinking what a lucky dude I was.

Startling me, she blurted out, "Farmer's market! Come on, let's go."

I laughed and got up to follow, but she began acting a little peculiar. She slowed down as she approached the door. Even her posture changed as she began tiptoeing, as though she were pretending to stalk something. When she got close to the door, she pounced on one of her flip-flops and said, "Got you!" She had stepped on the heel of her left flip-flop with her right foot, causing the toe end to stand up a little. Then she stuffed her left foot into it and said, "Ha!"

Amused, I stood and watched as she stepped on the heel of her right shoe.

"Ha!" She repeated, and stuffed her right foot into her other shoe.

When she noticed me trying not to laugh, she explained. "Yes, sometimes, that's how I put on my flip-flops. It's easier than trying to inch your way into them using your toes."

"Should I ever wear flip-flops, that's exactly how I'll put them on, but do I have to sneak up on them like that?"

She looked at me incredulously and assured me that I did. "Psh! YE-ah!"

"Well, okay then."

"And, *oh*! We are *so* getting you some flip-flops."

"Well, okay then!" Who was I to argue?

We went to the farmer's market, had lunch there, and then we both had a twenty-minute chair massage. It was a good day. Even the ringing in my ears was minimal. I should have been having a blast, but something about tomorrow was nagging at me. Hopefully, I was just nervous about walking into a den of killers and child predators. I didn't want my anxiety to be some kind of foreshadowing that my author friend would be sure to include in his next novel. We called him that evening though, and got him caught up.

Roger That

At 4 pm, Carla's car radio crackled. "We've been here for ten hours now. We might need to ask ourselves if they are going to show."

Carla pulled the mic off the dash and steeled herself into producing the most calming tone she could muster. "Patience. Everyone hold your positions and keep your eyes open, but someone bring Walt a burger or a slice of pie or something."

I snickered and stretched my legs.

Nearly three hours later, it was not just Walt who needed a burger. But finally, targets started showing up. Carla picked up her mic again. "Look alive, people! And just in case you haven't figured it out, it was supposed to be 7 *pm*, not 7 *am*. High alert! Shake it off and be ready."

Over the next ten minutes, four people from the moderately crowded New York street keyed a number into the security pad and slipped into the doorway we were watching.

Over the radio, someone reported, "The code is three-five-eight-five. I repeat, three-five-eight-five."

That dude has been watching too many cop shows.

Another voice announced, "Thermal imaging shows them going to the second floor, turning left, and then into a room on their right about twenty feet down. Someone is standing at the door letting them in. Unfortunately, that's where we lose them."

Perfect!

I put on my hat and picked up the jacket with the built-in button cam as I got out of the car. Thirteen hours of sitting in a bucket seat had made my legs and back stiff and uncomfortable. Joints popped as I slipped on the jacket. I hobbled a few steps while my circulation began to flow again. That nervous sensation returned deep in my chest and it was almost incapacitating. I steadied my nerves, suppressed my anxiety, and blended in with the rest of the pedestrians anyway. For a split second I considered walking past the door and postponing this encounter, but necessity reasserted itself so I peeled off and went into the same door as the others.

Through heavy static, someone on the task force asked, "Is that our guy?"

Irritated, Carla snapped into her mic, "Ignore him." She took the lack of response as compliance, but she noticed a man who had been using his phone in the next doorway snap his head around. Was he trying to get a good look?

Carla was on her radio again. "Who is in the next doorway? Is he one of ours?"

The hissing on the radio almost drowned out the voice that said, "Sergeant Brock here, NYPD. Tyler! Move out of the area." The man put his phone in his pocket as he walked away from the door in the opposite direction.

Once inside, I turned on my button cam. When I was upstairs, I took off my hat, rolled it up, and stuffed it into my back pocket as I approached the big brute by the door. To lure him into a false sense of security, I made sure he saw that my focus was purposefully down the hall, intentionally avoiding eye contact.

This is going to be tricky. I don't know how I'm going to be able to get in and out of there without taking anyone out. Somehow, I have to get through this without being forced to find a way to edit the video in this tiny video camera.

As I passed by the guy, I waited until I was sure he was no longer in the frame of the video before I focused on his neck. I did my best to catch him as he collapsed, but he probably weighed over two hundred pounds. The best I could do was slow him down. He made some noise as he hit the floor, but not enough for anyone inside to check on him. I stayed with him until I was sure he had passed out from a lack of oxygen.

The door was unlocked. I guessed that the brute was supposed to stop guys like me, and let in only the people who were expected.

Stepping into the condo was a rush. Not knowing what to expect from these dangerous people should have been frightening, but instead, it was exciting. Also, because I was unsure when the brute in the hall would regain consciousness, I couldn't waste a moment, although I took two seconds to lock the door behind me. At the very least, this would provide a warning when the brute woke up.

Outside, the thermal imaging guy on Carla's crackling radio reported my progress. "I don't know how he took out the guard so easily, but he's down and our guy is in."

Carla spoke into her mic. "He will probably be in there for a while. Go ahead and turn off thermal imaging."

"Roger that."

I'm Taking This Laptop

A man had the couch to himself, but because he was sitting on the edge of the cushion, only a small portion was being used. He was bent over a laptop on the coffee table, pointing at the screen and scolding someone. His Middle Eastern accent made it difficult to understand him, but he was clearly unhappy with an underling. When he noticed the eyes of all five of his minions had turned to me as I boldly approached them, he also looked up.

He and two others look like they could be from Syria, but Couch Boy seems to be in charge. I'm going to have to assume—

"Who the *hell* are you?" demanded the only one in the group who was standing.

The man I had presumed to be the Syrian slammed his laptop shut.

I moved into a position where no one was behind me and placed my hand over my heart as though it was intended to show sorrow, but I was simply covering the button cam. "Forgive me, but—"

The only guy standing pulled his gun, just as I had predicted. A quick, paralyzing glance in his direction caused him to hit the coffee table on the way to the floor. I kicked his gun under the couch.

So much for the fantasy of not having to edit this video, but at least it was just an audio edit. So far. In the back of my mind, I began considering how I could manage that on my phone.

"Sorry! Sorry. So, is anyone else armed?" Glancing around at shocked faces, I asked again, "No? Are you sure?" I pointed at one of them. "You? Are you armed?" He shook his head as the guy on the floor began to get up. "Okay, I would like to continue now. Like I was saying," Repositioning myself so that my button cam was pointing at who I thought was the Syrian, but did not include the guy getting up off the floor. When I uncovered the camera, I said in a low, calm voice, "please forgive the intrusion. As your largest competitor, *and* a loyal employee, I have a proposal."

"You don't even know what our business is."

I laughed good-naturedly even though I wanted to kill them all. Brutally.

"Heroin, prostitution, child pornography, human trafficking. Did I miss anything?"

Someone with a particularly low IQ spoke up. "Uh huh. Supplying marijuana to the medical dispensaries."

Everyone looked at him with contempt. He regretted opening his mouth and leaned back in his seat.

That must be his department.

"Right, and supplying marijuana to dispensaries." I looked at the Syrian and rolled my eyes, as though we were best buddies who were making fun of a schoolmate. "I have a proposition. I want out of this business because, frankly, I believe the feds are closing in on me and I don't have the manpower or infrastructure that you have."

The Syrian eyeballed me with narrow eyes, but I noticed his chest swelled with pride at the compliment I had given him. It should have been obvious to him that I was just trying to manipulate him. "How did you know I was here? Are you a cop?"

"Oh, I can assure you that I am not a cop. Like I said, I'm a member of your organization, sort of. That's how I knew about this meeting."

The Syrian's intense stare did not intimidate me. "Let me guess. Your proposition is to sell me something that already belongs to me, right?"

"No. I joined your organization after building a large database of the names and contact information for, well, people with questionable tastes. Your organization is larger than mine. You have content that I don't have, so when my customers ask for that content, I provide them links to your collection."

"What is your proposition, and why should I trust you?"

"I could have just walked in here and taken you all out, but I didn't because I want to do business with you."

He didn't appear to believe me, so I crossed my arms to cover my button cam and took the life of the man who had pulled the gun. He fell to the floor again. The troublemaker had been inching his way closer to me anyway, thinking he was being stealthy.

"Go ahead. Check for a pulse."

Someone did, and was shocked when he found none.

"How did you do that?"

"Careful planning." I didn't pause long enough for them to ask more questions. Before I uncrossed my arms, I turned so that the camera could not see the dead body, and pulled a 128GB USB flash drive out of my pocket. "My proposal is to sell you my distribution database of nearly fifty thousand paying customers, for one-point-five million dollars."

"Bah! That's ridiculous. I'm not giving you that much money for *anything*."

Any second now, the brute in the hall is going to wake up, or someone's going to notice him lying there.

"We're both businessmen here. Do the math. Each of these customers spends somewhere between ten and a hundred dollars a year, just on child porn."

The Syrian's eyes went up and to his left as he did the math, then his face softened as he nodded. "Let's say I pay you a million dollars—"

"A million and a half."

"—what then? We compete with each other?"

"No, *then* I retire to a South Pacific Island."

He looked at his minions. One shrugged and offered, "We *have* been hit hard."

The Syrian still appeared to be considering what to do but asked, "Can I see this data?"

I waved a hand at his laptop. "May I?"

He opened his laptop, typed in his password, and slid it over. I sat on the couch next to a vile man who tries to take as much money from Americans as possible while inflicting horrendous misery upon their children.

I could just kill these lowlifes right now and be done.

Using a text editor, I opened the XML file to reveal a fraction of the dummy data and turned the screen towards him so he could see.

"Can any of you use the data in this form?" The Syrian clearly had no IT experience. I rotated the laptop again so that the others could see. All but one looked confused by the XML tags, but the oldest of them affirmed that they could easily import the data.

Another IT Geek providing support for child porn? I should have killed him instead of the guy with the gun.

The Syrian reached for his computer and declared, "When we have the data imported, we will pay you your million dollars."

I closed the lid and tucked it under my left arm. "A million and a half, right now, or I walk. And I'm taking this laptop with me either way."

I can remote into my PC with this and edit the button cam video.

A few tense moments passed, but he said something to one of them in what I assumed was Dari or Arabic. One of the other Middle Eastern men got up and walked towards the bedroom.

"Woah. Where are you going? What are you doing?"

"He's getting your money. Do not kill him."

I followed him to the door but kept my eye on everyone, still trying to be cognizant of which way the button cam was pointing. I did *not* want the dead body on video. The man opened the closet and punched a code into a large safe.

The stress I had felt for days returned. I couldn't see the man's hands as he reached into the safe. He was pulling stacks of money out and putting it on the bed, but was there also a gun in the safe? Likely. I was watching him intently, but the others kept distracting me as they moved or shifted positions. I had to assume that every time the man reached into the safe, he'd pull out a gun and start shooting.

When his hands reached for the top shelf, rather than back to the bottom shelf where he had been retrieving the money, I focused on his neck and he collapsed.

Old School DOS Prompt

When the accountant fell over, the two stacks of fifty-dollar bills he had retrieved fell to the floor.

"Oh, sorry. Carry on."

Ugh. More to edit out.

It took him a moment to recover, but he finished counting.

"Put the money in a pillowcase."

He did, so I pulled the flash drive out of my new laptop and handed it to the Syrian, making sure the transfer was on video.

"Here. There are close to *fifty thousand* people in this distribution data who regularly watch child porn. You bought it, it's yours now, and I am out of the business and intend to retire."

He looked at me suspiciously but took the USB.

Got him, for sure.

I held the bag of money over my button cam while I told the Syrian, "I'm going to need you to throw that body down the stairwell to conceal the cause of death."

"What?"

"Just do it, and do it right now. It's in your best interest, too. How else are you going to explain his death?"

"Is my doorman dead, too?"

"No, he's just unconscious, and he's probably going to have a headache when he wakes up. You better drag him in to get him out of the hall. I'm sure you don't want people asking questions."

"My neighbors do not ask questions."

"Right."

Drawing their attention to the body in their living room, I repeated myself. "Now." I turned and threw the pillowcase of money over my right shoulder like Santa. Without even offering to help drag the Brute out of the hall, I stepped over him and hurried downstairs.

When I got to the first floor I whispered, "I think we got him," before turning off the button cam. But instead of exiting the building, I stepped into the condo's laundry room, which was a lucky convenience. The pillowcase of money could easily be mistaken for a load of dirty clothes.

I powered down the Syrian's laptop and turned it back on, but interrupted the boot process to start a DOS prompt. From there, I used the hotspot on my phone to remote into my laptop at Carla's apartment. Some decent video editing software made it easy to edit out the audio parts of the video that I did not want anyone else to hear.

The video portion was more-or-less acceptable, as I had blocked the view when needed. Altering the video portion would have been far more difficult because that would mean having to alter the time counter in the lower right corner, which would have taken hours. During the frames where the accountant had dropped some money after I focused on his neck, I edited the video by simulating a screen shake to lend some distracting ambiguity.

Editing took longer than I had hoped, but when the recording was as smooth and seamless as I could make it in the short amount of time available to me, I set the clock on my PC at home ahead five minutes and saved the video. I transferred the file to the laptop I took from the Syrian and uploaded it to the button cam from there.

Terminating the connections, I opened the log files, changed all the characters to zeroes, saved them, and then permanently deleted them. I powered down and hurried out of the building. When I dropped the bag of money, the laptop, and the video camera into Carla's car I simply said, "Make it stick."

As I walked off, I heard Carla on her radio again. "Block the exits and move in!"

(°o°)

Over the phone, Carla sounded mad. "Hey, there's only one point twenty-five million dollars here."

"Those bastards." My obvious sarcasm wasn't lost over on her end.

"Well?"

"'Well'? What do you mean 'well'? I just wanted to get the hell out of there. I didn't count it. You can see that on the video."

Carla barked at someone else, "Check the video."

She was probably in a place she couldn't speak freely. I wanted to ask her if she was okay but felt sure she wouldn't be able to answer honestly.

"I have way too much at stake to try to steal a quarter million dollars. On video."

After a few seconds of silence I asked, "Am I just supposed to be over here waiting, or what?"

"Hang on!" Now she was barking at me, too. It must be hectic in her office.

"Also, let's assume I *did* steal some money, which I didn't. But if I did, wouldn't our agreement clear me of any liability? It includes immunity for any crimes committed during the operation, right?"

"True."

"Just watch the video and count the money as it comes out of the safe. It's all there."

I could hear background noises over the phone, and Carla went on. "There also seems to be a time discrepancy between when you turned off the button cam and exited."

Thinking fast, I offered the best lie I could think of. "Well, I did stop at the door to wait for a lull in the foot traffic. Is that what they mean? Maybe I should have waited to turn off the cam?"

Then I realized something and that tightening stress deep in my chest returned.

"They are looking for some way to cancel my agreement, aren't they? Null and void."

She whispered, "Worse."

My head reeled. Hot anger swelled out of control and I could tell that my face was flushed.

Another whisper. "Far worse."

I thought for a moment, "Someone is trying to clear the Syrian. Someone on the inside. Who?"

No answer. I waited. Stress. Anger. Angrier. Another realization almost sent steam through my ears. "It's Assistant Director Jaris, isn't it?"

Her voice sounded shaky. "Okay, the money checks out. All the money is accounted for. Sorry for the confusion." Slowing down her pace in an obvious change, she added, "You. Are. Right."

And then she hung up.

He did seem a little eager to bring me into the fold. Friends close, enemies closer? But why didn't he just warn *the Syrian that we were coming?*

Carla did not get home until almost midnight, but was too livid to even try to sleep. "Under the ruse of preparing the case for trial, Jaris did everything he could to eliminate the video as evidence. That video is not just the most damning piece of evidence we have, the outcome of the case is *balanced* atop it."

She went on and on about the nonsense Jaris put them through. Non-stop venting for a good twenty minutes.

"Babe."

Although she stopped talking, I could tell her mind was still ruminating over the past several hours.

"Babe."

"What?" She whipped her head around to look at me as she nearly snapped my face off. She reminded me of that mean little dog that chewed on my pant leg.

What was that puppy's name? Sugar!

"Okay, Sugar, just listen to me for a minute."

The expression on her face changed, but I couldn't tell if it was irritation or surprise at being called "Sugar." I'd never called her that before. At first, I wondered if she'd get the reference, but then realized that if she did, she'd be livid *and* mad at me.

Distraction! I need a distraction. I'll get right to the point without the lead-in I'd prepared.

"Do you realize that the name Jaris originates in Syria?"

She stopped ruminating, and for a full three seconds her face looked like that little "surprised" emoji you can make with your phone's keyboard. (°o°) Her mouth was open in disbelief. Her head was thrown back and her eyes were wide with realization.

"Maybe Ken and I should talk to the attorney general's office tomorrow. They could get him suspended while we investigate him. Or at least recused from this case—"

"Okay, but wait a minute. What would happen to my immunity deal then? Right? *He* signed it."

"True, but now I'm wondering if he even filed it."

We tried to sleep, but we both tossed and turned most of the night. I fell asleep at some point because Carla woke me up making a phone call.

"...to call so early, I'll get right to the point. I think we might want to meet at the U.S. Attorney's office later." When she saw that I was awake, she motioned for me to be quiet. "What? You already made an appointment?" She looked back at me and made an imagine-that face. "Yeah, One Saint Andrews Plaza, nine o'clock."

Carla hung up without saying goodbye, like they do in the movies, and turned her attention to me. "Ken shares both your opinion and mine. He wants to transfer or duplicate your immunity deal with the U.S. Attorney General's office, and then talk to them about opening an investigation into Jaris."

The More You Have

"This evil, devious man was preying on our most vulnerable citizens. Our *children*. He forced untold numbers of girls *and boys* as young as *twelve or thirteen* into living lives as the sex slaves of anyone demented enough to pay the price. He made them believe the only reason they had a place to live or were able to eat at all was because only *he* would provide for them. He also made them believe that they were so worthless, no one else would want them." Ken made their case the best way he could with only a few hours to prepare.

"We don't *just* need this video submitted as evidence to prosecute this *horrendous* Syrian; we need our witness too. He is the one who infiltrated this organization and made the video. Without him, Jaris will get his way and have the evidence we need thrown out."

The assistant director for the U.S. Attorney still looked skeptical.

Carla also came prepared. She had a folder marked "Investigator's Eyes Only" in large, red print. "This folder contains photos of children as young as three years old. You do NOT want to see these photos, but I brought them just in case you had some doubt or reluctance."

The assistant director was still looking at the FBI agents in his cushy office chair as though he didn't believe them. "Give me that."

He opened the file and any hint of disbelief left his face. When he turned to the next page, the look of horror on his face was genuinely haunting. He closed the folder and whispered "I have grandchildren that age. This has to stop."

It took him a moment to recover, but the assistant director steeled himself and picked up his phone. "Guzman. I'm sending two distinguished FBI agents to your office. Stop whatever it is you're doing and give them everything they need for their investigation."

He stood, motioned them to the door, and spoke loud enough for his admin to hear him. "Cheryl, please escort our guests to Guzman's office and make sure they have everything they need."

"Yes, sir."

Talking back into the phone, he made his orders clear. "This is your highest priority until the prison doors slam shut on their perp, understand?"

He hung up and dashed out of his office, gesturing to Ken and Carla to follow.

"Here. Take some of Cheryl's cards. If you need anything, anything at all, you let her know." He handed them several business cards each, as though extra business cards meant they had more of his support.

Carla and Ken took the cards, but handed all but two back to Cheryl when they were down the hall.

"I've never seen him flustered like that. He's usually a hardass."

No Questions Asked

Three months blew by while we waited for the Syrian's trial. Three *months*.

With me in limbo.

Agreeing to the section of my immunity deal that said the video "must lead to an arrest and conviction" had been a grievous mistake. All I could do was hide and wait. I couldn't take out other criminals for fear of committing a crime outside of our agreement with the attorney general. We should have known the trial would take months. I couldn't even leave the house without wearing things to hide my face from watchful eyes and camera systems that might have facial recognition software.

No charges were filed against Jaris. They couldn't make anything stick although he was politely asked to resign when charges *were* filed against his admin. Carla suspected that he set up his admin because she was close enough for him to frame her. He may have even hired her because she was Middle Eastern, so his frame job would be more believable, even though she wasn't Syrian.

Carla's and Ken's immovable boss was only able to move in one direction. Up. He took Jaris' place as Assistant Director and Ken moved up to the head of their department.

Then one Monday afternoon in mid-July, out of the blue, the Syrian changed his plea to guilty. We wouldn't even have to go to trial! A new prosecutor offered him a plea deal that they didn't think he would accept, but he did. It made everyone wonder what else might have come out in the trial. Or maybe he just wanted to avoid capital punishment.

Didn't matter. What *did* matter was that it brought my immunity deal *and* my entry into the witness protection program into question, again. The prosecutor argued that the video played no part in the conviction and it was his expertise and efforts that had sealed the plea deal.

Carla, Ken and I all interpreted it as the prosecution wanting to take full credit for the arrest and conviction, *and* go after me for the crimes I'd committed. Ken made a phone call.

"Cheryl?"

"Yes?"

"FBI Agent Ken Starnes here. Agent Carla Bright and I spoke to you about three months ago. Do you remember me?"

"Yes, of course. You were here about the Syrian."

"Exactly. Sorry to bother you, but we need help."

Ken explained the situation to Cheryl, who started a satisfying chain reaction. She told her boss when he returned from a meeting, who called Guzman, who paid a visit to the prosecutor, who subsequently resigned in haste.

Guzman took over and put the whole ordeal to bed. He finalized my deal himself by adding an addendum that included the possibility of a plea deal. I actually met him in his office, face to face, although Carla accompanied me. I wore a hat and dark sunglasses, but not because of a lack of trust. It was more disbelief. I did not want to walk into a federal office and set off facial recognition software. It might take days or even months for Carla to get me out of jail.

Cheryl escorted us to Guzman's office, who was already flipping through the paperwork of my agreement. "Come in. Sit down, Agent Bright aaaaand..."

Instead of answering, I asked, "The agreement is filed, right? The government can't change its mind? You can't get mad and recall it, or tear it up to render it null and void or anything like that? It's a done deal, without any exceptions?"

"That's right, just like I said on the phone. It's a fresh start for you, or for whoever this agreement is intended, anyway."

I was becoming even more suspicious of intentions and loopholes.

Guzman could tell I was growing impatient, even with my dark sunglasses, and went on. "How do I know you are the person for which this document is intended? The places where there are supposed to be a name and Social Security number are blank. *Any*one could write *any*thing in there."

I tilted my head in response. "Okay, that's a good point, but I'm the one who wanted it done that way, to protect my interests."

Carla chimed in, "It's him. I've been working with him for years, so I would know. This man saved countless children *and* prevented tons of cocaine and heroin from filtering into our streets. He accomplished what several law enforcement agencies could not do for years. *Decades*. We owe him."

While he shrugged sympathetically, Guzman let us know the problem was not yet solved by pointing to the blanks in the agreement.

I had an idea. "Can I make a suggestion that works out better for all of us?"

"By all means."

"Do the witness protection paperwork first. Assign me my new name and Social Security number, and we'll fill in the blanks on the immunity deal with that."

He chuckled but seemed open to the idea. "For lack of a better solution," he tried to look me in the eye, but couldn't see through the dark shades I was still wearing, "and for our deep appreciation of your services to aid humanity and law enforcement efforts, I will grant your request. What name should we use?"

Carla turned to me as if to ask, "Yeah?"

I had thought about it long and hard, but hated every name I'd considered. They all *sounded* as made up as they were, but one day while Carla was at work, I slipped away for a fancy lunch at the ancient baths and spa place on Franklin Street. After having Pistachio Shell Paper Encrusted Prawns for lunch (yes, seriously) I slipped into a hot tub to coax the stress away. I was not even thinking about what my new name could be. The idea just came to me.

My last name could be my maternal grandmother's maiden name. The last name of the man who built my family's cabin.

Smith. The most common surname in America, which would help me to remain anonymous, too.

To even things out, I decided on the first name of my other maternal great grandfather, Anthony, which is also a very common name. For a middle name, I just did an Internet search for names that go with Anthony and came up with James.

But I didn't explain any of that to them. I just said, "Anthony James Smith. I could go by Tony!"

Carla's amused expression morphed into disbelief. "*Tony*? Seriously? You don't look anything like a Tony."

"Huh? Wait, what? What does a Tony look like?"

"Well, not you."

Guzman chuckled again. "Should I give you two a moment?"

She sighed. "Whatever. That's fine."

I know what she's thinking right now. She is thinking that she's just going to call me 'babe,' anyway.

"Okay, I'll submit this, but it'll take a few minutes for them to get back to me with a Social Security number."

He pecked some data into his computer, then asked, "What is the property you need back, and do you have any idea where it might be, or who, uh, who confiscated it?"

"Let me first remind you that this agreement states, 'no questions asked.'"

Raised eyebrows and a slight head tilt proceeded his reply. "Well, okay. I get it, it's not my place to ask."

"Seriously now, the time for questions has come and gone. All of us, together, struck this agreement and it says riiiiight *there*, 'no questions asked.'" I pointed to the words.

"No questions. Got it."

I helped myself to the pad of sticky notes on his desk and wrote down the address of my cabin.

"Oh, *property*. I thought I'd be getting something from an evidence locker. This might take a few minutes while I figure this out."

"That's okay. We are just waiting anyway."

Guzman pecked away on his computer for nearly half an hour, occasionally making a frustrated face, but then looked disgusted. "Wait, do you mean the estate confiscated from a *serial ki—*?"

"Bup, bup, bup, bup! No questions asked." I had expected some resistance.

"But I ca—"

"Bup! No. Questions. Asked."

"But—"

"BUP!" Yes, I was trying to annoy him with my "bups."

Carla intervened. "May I explain?"

Leaning back, Guzman rubbed the back of his neck with one hand but kept his other hand near his phone as though he would snatch it at any moment and call his boss. "Please."

"First, *alleged* serial killer. The FBI may have acted in haste when it seized that estate and froze the accounts of his employees. The people we thought our suspect had killed were indeed deceased, however, no cause of death could be found. In any of them. There is no proof any of the *victims* were actually murdered, so there is not even any credible *evidence* that he killed anyone. It was all circumstantial and it would be just as easy, or as difficult, to blame those deaths on you or me as it would him."

Oh, she is good.

"No cause of death? They all just died in his presence? Maybe he poisoned them."

Carla snapped her finger and became sarcastic. "Poison! Of course. *Why* didn't we think of that?"

Guzman looked a little humiliated.

She went on. "There was no poison. He wasn't even anywhere near most of them when they died, and he'd never encountered any of them before. It was all just tragically circumstantial."

No, seriously, she is good.

He still looked skeptical.

"Again, without a cause of death, no one could even prove they were murdered. Why would we look for a murderer when no one was even murdered?"

When Guzman looked at me, I added, "She's not lying."

It took hours to complete the paperwork and get it signed and filed, but when we finished, Carla and I had lobster for dinner.

Over dessert and coffee, Carla smiled her devilish little smile again and whispered, "See? An immunity deal. Easy."

Decaf nearly spurted out of my nose.

Weeks passed before they could arrange to have the deed to my cabin transferred back. When it was finally time to sign the paperwork, I did not put it back in my name. Either of my names. I had contacted the only relative I was aware of, which was a once-removed, second cousin who I remembered from my youth. We only saw each other while attending family reunions, but we always got along.

All of our older generation relatives had passed on over the years, but I'd kept in contact with her. Just enough to stay in touch, but she seemed decent. She was a nurse at a hospital in Denver and a mother of three. Hopefully, she would be able to keep the cabin in the family for multiple generations.

I did not want to risk blatantly moving the money out of my Steven Andrews alias investment account. I didn't want anyone saying I had broken a law by keeping the money I had taken from drug dealers. I had been granted immunity for taking the cash, but keeping it might be seen differently. So, I opened a crowdfunding account called "Save the Geeks!" Donations would help IT folks who had been hit hard by layoffs.

Two people made legitimate donations. Thank you, new friends.

Moving millions of dollars from my aliased account to the crowdfunding campaign was *too* easy. Over a short amount of time, the money was automatically deposited into my legitimate "Tony" account, and I closed the "Save the Geeks!" campaign.

Quite the Agenda

Just to see what would happen, I counted out three-quarters of a million bucks from the leftover drug dealer money and took it to a small, local bank. Carla was pleased that I resisted going through the drive-thru with all that cash. We brought along my new driver's license, my new Social Security number, and my immunity deal agreement, in case they asked where I got the money.

"I'd like to open a new account."

The teller gasped when I opened my bag and showed her deep stacks of fifty and one-hundred dollars bills.

"Oh, sir, I'll have to get my supervisor."

I gasped a little, opened my eyes wide, and put my hand over my mouth as though getting a supervisor was a big deal.

A silver-haired woman with an intricate hairdo and a business suit and jacket asked us to come into her office.

"Where did you get all this cash?"

"Saved it. I started out just stickin' coins in a sock. Kept it under my bed."

She looked at me, waiting for more, so I nodded quickly while continuing to smile. She looked at Carla next, who was embarrassed and slowly shaking her head.

"I'm going to have to contact th—"

Carla must have anticipated this reaction and already had her hand on her badge. She whipped it out. It's good to have your own FBI agent handy. When the supervisor seemed satisfied, Carla looked at me and said, "I *told* you to wear your suit."

I shrugged and nodded, trying to appear as though I was submitting to the fact that she was right, but inside I was laughing. *I love it when she plays along.*

The supervisor continued looking at us like we were crazy. When she took too long to respond, I asked, "Are we good? Or should I go to the credit union down the street?"

"Tell you what, I'm going to get someone in here to start counting all that while I contact a district manager."

"No need, it's three-quarter-million even, I trust you."

Carla let a sigh accompany her shaking head and embarrassment.

"Sir, I, we'll, need to—"

"I'm kidding! Count it. I admire you for wanting to multitask. You recognize that we are both busy people and you're trying to perform tasks simultaneously to accomplish goals faster. You rock."

She stood, pulled the bottom of her jacket down like Captain Picard, and stepped to her open office door. "Karla?"

Carla turned around. "Yes?"

The supervisor looked at her and asked, "Huh?"

Carla pointed out of the door and said, "Oh, you, your—"

Her silver hairdo bounced as she chuckled nervously and said, "Yes, she, her—"

They were both thankful when Karla walked up. "How can I help?"

She pointed to the bag of money and said, "Please begin counting the money in that bag. We'll need to count it three times. I'll be back in a few minutes."

Karla began counting, stacking, and writing notes to herself. She stopped for a moment to smell a stack of bills and remarked, "All this money smells like," she sniffed again, "clothesline fresh."

Carla grinned and said, "Oh, thrifty shopper, eh?"

I leaned close to Carla and whispered, "Putting in the dryer sheets was a really good idea, thanks!" We had literally laundered the money. Carla knew to remove traces of drugs, or even explosives, because of the source of all the cash. Wet money does not smell good, so Carla tossed in a handful of the "Clothesline Fresh" scented dryer sheets she had purchased on sale.

The supervisor returned, looking satisfied. "The district manager says the word of the FBI is good enough for him. Where are we?"

I gave Carla an extended, impressed nod of approval. She rolled her eyes.

Carla must have the most toned eyeball muscles on the planet.

"Just started the second count."

"Ok, finish up and I'll count the third."

We sat in silence, not wanting to disturb her.

"Uh oh." Karla had bad news. "Both times I counted seven hundred and fifty thousand, *and fifty* dollars."

"Whaaaa?"

Carla gave me another one of her looks. "You did that on purpose, didn't you?"

"I just wanted to see if they'd pocket it."

The woman in the business suit had a scowl on her face. I don't think she approved of my humor and tactics. "You had quite the agenda today, didn't you?"

"Sorry. Should I just go to the credit union down the street?"

If looks could kill.

Oh, hmmm.

Into the Sunset

With Ken getting the top spot in the department, the Syrian behind bars, and Qian extradited to Lithuania, Carla decided to take a leave of absence from the FBI. She didn't really need to work anyway. We had enough money to last the rest of our lives, even if all we did was sell a few of our diamonds every year. Also, in just ten months, those cryptocurrency investments had taken off like a social media lie. My profit on that sale had been over six hundred percent.

Life was good. And the future was wide open.

Carla could easily retire but opted for a temporary leave to give herself options. She was too used to working and making a difference was important to her. For that, she had my highest respect.

After sleeping late, we sat at our table by the window and watched people as we talked.

"I seem to be drinking more Earl Grey and less coffee lately."

"Yeah, I noticed. I like this." She sipped hers after she added a touch of honey.

"Less stress?"

"Maybe."

I thought for a moment. "Are we drinking more tea because we are less stressed, or are we less stressed because we are drinking less coffee?"

"Oh, don't be dissing my coffee. I'm still loyal to my beans, I just like a little tea now and then." She sighed. "You know, I just don't know what to do with myself right now. I've always had either work or school."

"You don't seem to be enjoying your first day of leave, and you're only an hour and a half into it. Why don't we jump on a plane and go see our author friend? Get him caught up."

"Can we do that? Just get on a plane?"

"Absolutely! And now that I *can*, I want to."

Early the next morning we stood in front of the TSA agent who had taken our driver's license and tickets. He was smiling and in a good mood because it was still early, but when he scanned my new license, he frowned.

Oh, good, grief. What now?

Carla and I were concerned, but we just waited silently to see what would happen. The TSA agent waved someone over, but it was taking a while for the other agent to make his way through the crowd, so he set my things aside and processed Carla's. That was a good sign, or at least a better sign than the trouble he was giving me.

The TSA agent looked at Carla. "Ma'am?"

I cringed, hoping Carla would let that go.

"Go ahead and go through the security line."

We both knew that was a strategic play to separate us and *not* an effort to make the security process more efficient, so Carla opened up her jacket and showed him the badge clipped to her belt. "I'll wait here, thanks."

The second agent arrived and the first agent pointed to his screen and asked, "What does that warning mean? I've never seen that."

"FPID."

The first agent looked at him and gave him a still-don't-know shrug.

"Federal Protection ID."

"Oh."

"And now the general public knows we know, thanks to you."

So, my identification is not completely anonymous. That's good to know, but bad practice. Extraordinarily bad practice. The group of people who know I am in a witness protection program is supposed to be tiny, but it is not. The number of privy people is exponentially bigger than I thought.

Using a simple "follow me" gesture of his head, the second agent escorted us around the long lines of the x-ray machines and into the terminal.

"Have a safe flight."

A peace offering? A bribe?

Six hours later we were in and out of Denver, driving a luxury SUV west on I-70. When we got into the foothills we exited and drove through some of the most beautiful autumn leaves I'd seen in years. My author friend's new place was something between living in a neighborhood and living in the country. The neighbors weren't close, but there were still sidewalks and white picket fences.

There were deer in his front yard when we drove up. Seven of them. They watched us as we got out of the car and knocked on his door, but then went back to munching on his lawn.

We talked for hours, ordered pizzas for a late lunch, and talked some more. Carla received a text after all the pizza was gone. She read it and exclaimed, "Yes!" She had our attention.

"Both of you are going to want to hear this." Carla dialed a number on speakerphone and motioned for us to be quiet with a finger to her lips.

"Hello?" I recognized the voice immediately but kept quiet, as Carla had indicated.

"Jeanna! This is Special Agent Bright."

"Agent Bright! Hello! Are... are you calling with good news or bad news?"

"I have good news, bad news, and more good news. Which do you want first?"

"Well, the good news-es, of course."

"Your accounts are being released."

You could hear the relief in Jeanna's voice. "Oh, thank goodness. I want one of those new electric cars so bad I already miss the gas stations."

"The other good news is, your old boss is no longer a suspect. He's not wanted for *any*thing."

"Thank goodness. He didn't seem to be the type for that kind of thing."

Carla handed me the phone. I wished I'd had a couple more minutes to think of what to say to her. "Jeanna?"

"Oh! Hello. You're there. Are you okay? What was all that about? I'm sorry I sold the business. They made an offer I could not turn down. And you weren't there, and I hadn't heard from you in months, and I couldn't handle it by myself. And I felt like I just swooped into the business you created and sold it out from under you, and—"

Laughing, I had to interrupt. "Jeanna! You did the right thing. I'd have sold it too. Besides, it was *you* who turned that business into a money-maker, not me. You absolutely made the right decision."

"That makes me happy."

"You are quite the businesswoman. Hopefully, you'll take some of that money and open up another business."

"Yes! Can we do that? Can we open a business together?"

"Well, that brings up the bad news Carla mentioned."

"The bad news? Are you okay?"

"Yes, I'm fine, thank you. It seems I have to go into a federal witness protection program though, and will be gone again."

"What? Why?"

"Permanently this time."

"Oh." Jeanna didn't even try to hide her disappointment.

"But Jeanna, you can totally open a new business by yourself. You turned a shell of a company into *millions* of dollars. *You* did that, not me, and you can do it again."

"Really? Do you think so?"

"Yes. And go get that plug-in."

We said a long goodbye and hung up.

After our author friend was all caught up and we were ready to leave, he was shocked when we gave him a cashier's check for a half-million dollars.

"Use this to produce a movie or a new TV series based on your trilogy of our adventures."

"I will! I've already had a couple of nibbles. People might be interested in seeing all this. It's a binge-worthy series I'd watch, for sure."

"Looking forward to it."

We said more goodbyes, but I couldn't promise to stay in touch. He waved from his front porch as we drove directly into the bright, Colorado sun. I was trying to block the sunlight from my eyes so that I could see down the long driveway, but suddenly busted out laughing.

Carla was looking around, trying to figure out what I was laughing about. "What's so funny?"

"From his perspective, we are riding off into the sunset."

Carla chuckled. "You are *so* easily amused."

"Yeah. It's true. So. Carla. How do you feel about checking in on my cousin and her kids at my— at *their* cabin, and then going to Bristlecone Springs to meet a friend of mine?"

"Okay."

"You know, Bristlecone Springs has some of the best hot springs in the Rocky Mountains."

"Yeah? I could do some hot springs. I'll find us a coupon."

Millions in the bank, but she still looks for coupons. "*Love* you!"

"Love you too."

We drove off into the brilliant orange sunset, surrounded by the soothing greens of pines, bright yellow, autumn aspen groves, and deer calmly grazing on golden mountain grasses.

Afterword

I did my best to tell the story of "Tony" as he told it to me, without revealing enough details for the criminals they had targeted to find them, or even recognize them. I call him Tony now because I still do not know his given name. Despite being friends with him for years, and knowing more about him than anyone else except for "Carla," I *still* don't know his name.

And I have no idea where they went when they *literally* rode off into the sunset. Did they start a whole new life using his new, government-issued identification? Or did they take their millions in cash and diamonds and retire to Happy Valley-Goose Bay? Or did they take a permanent vacation at their favorite Old English resort? Maybe they accepted Chip's invitation to visit him in "Bristlecone Springs."

That's not the real name of that quaint little town, of course, but if someone were willing to travel around and visit the teahouses in many of the small towns dotting the Rocky Mountains, they might recognize the back deck where Chip and Shannon met. I visited the establishment once and sat at the table where he first joined her for tea so that I could more accurately portray the beauty and coziness of that special place. If you find that teahouse, keep your eyes open around town for one or two inseparable couples.

I have to say that, to me, their story is simply not complete. Not only are there too many horrible people left out there to deal with, but I also feel *certain* that "Qian" will be free one day.

But until then...

The end.

As the Credits Roll

A lot of people like to stay and watch the credits roll after the movie has ended. That's not for everyone, I get that. Most people want to rush away to try to beat the crowd out of the theater and the parking lot. But there are still a few of us who like to stay until the lights come up. I love it when the movie includes little tidbit bonuses while the credits are rolling, like behind-the-scenes photos, bloopers and deleted scenes. *Ferris Bueller* had my all-time favorite credits.

Right now, some of my cherished readers might be thinking, "this isn't a movie!" Well, it's not on the screen *yet*, but still, I feel like I need to add something similar here, so please try to imagine credits rolling in the foreground.

Work with me here. And be sure to cue the music in your head.

I'm not sure if this is frustrating or funny, but after all the editing was finished and I was working on the final formatting and ad campaign for the release of this novel, *two days* from publishing, an online news article grabbed my attention while I was eating lunch. In a time when there is so much fake news out there, it's difficult to know what's real, but this article seemed legit. Near Blue River, Colorado, three criminals were found dead, all together in a heap, as though they dropped dead where they stood.

The part that got my attention though, and what made me think this story was significant, was the fact that no cause of death could be determined. All three had extensive prior records, yet they had no weapons on them. They were found beside the entrance to an underground, well-ventilated meth lab, where they were also producing their own acetone.

Authorities theorized that maybe the ventilation system had stopped working and they had to evacuate the lab, but were overcome with acetone fumes. If two of them were helping the other out, this scenario might explain why they were all found piled together. It was also a couple of hours before a neighbor noticed them, which gave the acetone in their lungs time to dissipate.

Uh huh. Yeah. I'm *sure* that's what killed them.

Anyway, when I published The Attunement back in 2013, which was the first novel in this trilogy, something similar happened. "Tony" contacted me a couple of days after the book had been published, so it was too late to alter that one. This time, I read that article in time to include this one last note before publishing, so you'd know he's probably still out there somewhere, trying to make the world a better place.

You're welcome.

Okay! Let's roll. (The credits.)

The end?

COME VISIT *Bristlecone Springs'*
NATURAL HOT SPRINGS AT THE

Hot Springs Pools

A SOURCE OF RELAXATION, EXHILARATION,
AND NATURAL HEALING WATERS

AND RECEIVE

20% OFF

ANY SOAK OF YOUR LIKING

LIMIT ONE COUPON PER CUSTOMER

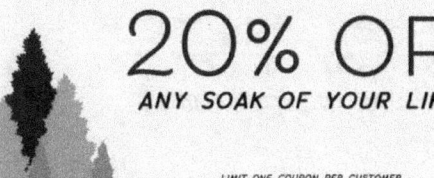

ALL INN

── HOTEL & CASINO ──
GOOD FOR

1 FREE NIGHT

LIMIT ONE COUPON PER CUSTOMER • CERTAIN RESTRICTIONS MAY APPLY

ALL INN

── HOTEL & CASINO ──
BOOK A WEEK'S STAY AT THE HOTEL AND RECEIVE

$100 CREDIT AT THE CASINO

LIMIT ONE COUPON PER CUSTOMER

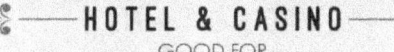

COME VISIT *Bristlecone Springs'*
NATURAL HOT SPRINGS AT THE

Hot Springs Pools

A SOURCE OF RELAXATION, EXHILARATION,
AND NATURAL HEALING WATERS

AND RECEIVE

20% OFF

ANY SOAK OF YOUR LIKING

LIMIT ONE COUPON PER CUSTOMER

ALL INN

—— HOTEL & CASINO ——

GOOD FOR

1 FREE NIGHT

LIMIT ONE COUPON PER CUSTOMER • CERTAIN RESTRICTIONS MAY APPLY

ALL INN

—— HOTEL & CASINO ——

BOOK A WEEK'S STAY AT THE HOTEL AND RECEIVE

$100 CREDIT AT THE CASINO

LIMIT ONE COUPON PER CUSTOMER

www.ingramcontent.com/pod-product-compliance
Lightning Source LLC
Chambersburg PA
CBHW071120170626

46809CB00002B/437